Filthy
Rich
Part 2

Kendall Banks

Life Changing Books in conjunction with Power Play Media
Published by Life Changing Books
P.O. Box 423 Brandywine, MD 20613

Library of Congress Cataloging-in-Publication Data;
www.lifechangingbooks.net
13 Digit: 9781934230527

Follow Us:

Twitter: www.twitter.com/lcbooks

Facebook: Life Changing Books

Instagram: @lcbooks

Pinterest: Life Changing Books

Also By Kendall Banks

Filthy Rich Part One

One Night Stand Part One

Another One Night Stand

Welfare Grind Parts 1-4

Rich Girls

www.lifechangingbooks.net

Chapter-1

The woods surrounding the cabin on the far outskirts of Montgomery County were still and serene. The afternoon sun shined brightly from the sky almost blindingly. Birds chirped from the branches of countless towering trees in what seemed like unison. Deer drank from a nearby racing river, its clear water revealing the rock covered floor filled with fish.

Obviously the woods were a far cry from the violence and plague filled streets of the inner city of Washington D.C. so many miles away. Problems and ulterior motives had no place here. There were no wars over drugs, cold stares and fighting over territory. There were no mothers crying over children who'd lost their lives senselessly. There were no gunshots and screams.

Or were they?

"Ahhhhhhhhhhhhhhhhhhhh!!!!!"

The shrieking and ear piercing scream erupted from the cabin out of nowhere. It echoed loudly against the trunks of each tree. Out of place, it caused the woods to stand even more still than before. Birds seemed to cease chirping immediately. The squirrels seemed to end their mission for the moment and the deer raised their heads from the river.

Everything fell still.

No movement.

Silence.

Then...

"Ahhhhhhhhhhhhhhhhhhhhhhhhhh!!!!!"

The scream erupted once again, this time more agony filled than before. In fact, there was something far beyond agony in its tone and volume, something that made it sound as if a horrible act was being inflicted. Something that a rational human being wouldn't wish on their worst enemy. It seemed to be filled with a brutal torment.

Moments passed.

"Ahhhhhhhhhhhhhhhhhhhhhhhhhhhhhh!!!!!"

Flocks of birds released from the branches of the trees and flew into the sky, the flapping of their wings hard and loud, their numbers blocking out the sun for a brief moment. The squirrels dashed in all directions. The deer leapt over the river and quickly disappeared into the surrounding trees never looking back.

As another scream erupted along with what appeared to be loud crying and whimpering, a sort of grim darkness seemed to blanket the woods. It wasn't the darkness of a setting sun though. It was more like the darkness given off at cemeteries during someone's passing, during the moment a dead body is discovered by a loved one...

The darkness that signaled death.

In the basement of the cabin, Trinity was bent over a wooden table with her hands tied tightly behind her back. The rope around her wrists was so tight they were ripping into her flesh. Her hair was matted and sprawled wildly all over her face. Both of her eyes were nearly swollen shut. Blood leaked from the gash over her left eye. Her lips were swollen and chapped.

"Take the dick, bitch!" a man screamed as he roughly forced his throbbing erection into Trinity's rectum.

"Ahhhhhhhhhhhhhhhhhhh!!!!!" Trinity screamed.

Trinity had never felt pain like what she was experiencing at the moment. In fact, the word *pain* was an understatement. It couldn't truly describe the hurt. Her anus was literally being ripped and torn. She could feel it. It felt like fire. She

2

could even feel herself bleeding. She could even feel herself nearing a bowel movement.

"Take it!" the rapist demanded once again as he gripped her hips so hard his nails dug deeply into the skin of Trinity's hips drawing blood. As he pounded her, his pants were down around his ankles. "Take it all, bitch!"

Tears streamed down Trinity's battered face from her swollen eyes without end. She hurt much more than just physically. She hurt emotionally and spiritually. She felt like something far more than just her sex was being taken from her. Something far more than just her body was being raped.

For the past several days, Trinity had been mercilessly beaten and raped. She hadn't been fed or given water. Her entire body was now aching terribly from the abuse. She was weak and her mouth utterly dry. Her stomach felt as if it were touching her spine.

Trinity wanted to die.

"Damn, this ass is tight!" the goon yelled, enjoying every second of what he was inflicting.

More thrusts.

Trinity saw her mother's face inside her head. After all, it was Chetti who had given the order to rape and kill her. It was her own flesh and blood who was responsible for her suffering. She was the entire reason. Something beyond hatred brewed inside Trinity now for Chetti. There was also disappointment though. Of course she knew Chetti was heartless. Of course she knew her mother would possibly have her killed or tortured if it came down to it. Still though, a piece of Trinity had always held out hope that maybe she was wrong, that maybe her mother had some sort of compassion inside her that she kept concealed for her only daughter. She now knew she was wrong. She now hated herself along with her mother for giving the old heartless bitch even the tiniest morsel of the benefit of the doubt.

The rapist's thrusts continued.

Trinity's tears continued to fall.

The slapping sounds of colliding thighs continued to

3

echo off the walls.

The man panted and sweated profusely as he stroked. Wiping sweat from his brow, he continued to grip his victim's hips while looking down at both her ass and the blood covering his erection. He smiled sickly as he continued to inflict damage and pain. He purged on Trinity's suffering like a vampire on blood. He couldn't get enough of it.

Trinity continued to cry loudly, her stomach and chin pressed closely against the surface of the tabletop. As she did, her mind drifted back to a moment from her past, a memory she'd barricaded somewhere in the darkest corner of her mind. The rapist's thrusts and strokes forced her body to rock back and forth so hard the bottoms of the table's legs shrieked loudly against the surface of the grime covered floor, Trinity heard her father's voice, "That's daddy's little girl," he whispered in her ear, his body on top of her young body so close she could barely breathe.

Trinity could remember her father molesting her. She could still feel the pain of his thick erection tearing her young virgin vagina mercilessly as he pushed all of himself deeply inside her. She could still feel herself leaking blood and staining the bed sheets underneath her. It all seemed so fresh, so vivid.

"Take all of daddy," Mr. Bishop whispered into his daughter's ear as he pushed into her so hard the headboard repeatedly banged against the wall. "That's my good girl. Daddy's baby."

Trinity could still remember the salty and bitter taste of countless tears as they found their way from her eyes to her mouth. She felt so betrayed, so let down. It killed her inside to have her own father taking something away from her so sacred, so cherished; something a father was supposed to teach his daughter to hold onto for as long as possible. It was heartbreaking.

"That's it, baby," Chetti's voice appeared. "Introduce her to womanhood."

Chetti spoke those words as she sat right beside the act;

4

naked. Sitting beside her daughter and husband on the bed, she rubbed Trinity's head softly as she urged her husband on. Her daughter's tears meant nothing to her. Trinity wanted to spaz out at the thought but her reminiscing on the past was cut short.

"You fuckin' ,slut!" the goon yelled, bringing Trinity back to reality. "Take this dick like a nasty bitch!"

Harder thrusts.

Trinity screamed. The pain was unbearable. Along with pain though, fury fueled inside her. If there was a God, a God who would somehow get her out of this, she swore with everything inside her she was going to slice her rapist's dick off and make him choke on it.

Moments passed.

The door at the top of the stairs opened.

Footsteps began to make their way down.

Trinity didn't bother to look towards the steps. She already knew who was coming. For the past several days she'd been shared by two men. The man now making his way down the steps was her present rapist's partner.

A thud sounded, a thud that sounded like a body forced to the floor.

Trinity still didn't look.

"Got a surprise for you, bitch," the goon who'd just come down the steps said. "One you might like."

Trinity ignored the tall, lanky man who wore a patch over one eye. Her body still continued to rock back and forth from the pounding behind her.

"Look, bitch!"

"You hear the nigga talkin' to you," the man behind Trinity said, snatching her by the hair and forcing her face towards the far wall. His breath was horrific and smelled like last week's trash. Bile rose up in her stomach as she kept her eyes closed tightly.

"Open your eyes, bitch!" he shouted. "You gon' make me fuck you up some more," he threatened.

Trinity opened her eyes as far as she could which wasn't

much. The swelling around them made opening them beyond just narrow slits difficult. Her vision was also blurry. The blood that dripped into her left eye was adding to it also. Still though, she forced herself to look. It took several moments for her eyes to focus. When they did, she couldn't believe them. What or *who* she was seeing sitting on the floor just couldn't be real.

Both goons laughed.

The man sitting on the floor looked far beyond haggard. His afro was heavily matted. His face was dirty. His chin was buried in his chest, saliva falling from his mouth. His pajamas were dirty and soiled with urine. Still, underneath it all, Trinity recognized him.

It was Cedrick.

In disbelief, Trinity's eyes wouldn't leave her brother, the man she'd thought was dead.

Laughing and now approaching Trinity, the man with the patch over his eye; the one who'd pushed Cedrick down the steps said, "Just wanted to give the two of y'all muthafuckas a quick family reunion before the funeral." He paused to dig deeply into his nose with his forefinger before heading toward Trinity.

"… Wanted to let his sorry ass see his sister get fucked real good one last time before we kill her."

Trinity ignored his words. She could only see her brother at the moment.

Reaching Trinity, the dirty bastard pulled out his gun. He then unzipped his pants, pulled out his dick and said, "Do a good job sucking this dick, bitch. If you bite, I'll blow your fuckin' head off."

Trinity didn't want to.

She began shaking her head from side to side.

The tears began to flow even more than before.

"Now!" he ordered.

A part of Trinity still wanted to die. A part of her wanted to defy him so he would go ahead and splatter her brains all over the place. Another part of her didn't want to die, not now that

6

she knew her brother was alive.

"Do it, ho!"

Trinity finally did as she was told. With her assailant's pants now down to his knees she dropped to the floor and stuffed his limp dick into her mouth.

"That's a good bitch," he said, watching Trinity go to work.

Trinity found herself gagging and choking on the goon's shaft as he forced himself deeply into her mouth so far the tip of his head was touching the back of her throat as the other goon commenced to pounding her from behind.

What seemed like forever passed.

So many thrusts.

So many moans and groans.

Both men changed positions.

More thrusts.

More laughter.

More of Trinity's screams.

As it continued, Cedrick remained on the floor with his eyes closed and his chin buried in his chest. Saliva continued to fall from his mouth and drench his pajama shirt. He didn't move or speak.

Then...

Cedrick's eyes opened. His head arose slowly. Without saying a word, he watched in silence as his sister was being raped a distance away from him. With his eyes locked on the brutality and with no one paying the slightest attention to him, he reached slowly behind him and pulled a gun from underneath his shirt.

The moment had come for Cedrick to reveal himself.

Cedrick had spent the past several months allowing everyone to think he was still under the spell of the drugs his mother had been giving him. In reality though, the moment when he secretly flushed the pills for the first time, he hadn't taken any more of them since. It had been a difficult road for him. Staying off the pills seemed impossible at times. They had

7

clouded his mind for so long and had been so much a part of his life that his body craved them like food and water. Going without them caused his body to go into heavy withdrawal. He threw up constantly. His body shook. Yet, he fought it. He fought every day to stay off them.

Eventually, he won.

Keeping his newfound state of mind secret, Cedrick listened as his mother told the two goons who were now raping Trinity to bring him to the cabin. She'd discovered that Nessa knew about Cedrick. To keep him from being found, she ordered them to bring him to the cabin until further notice. They had also been ordered to kill Trinity. Cedrick didn't know who Nessa was. All he knew was that the goons didn't do exactly what Chetti had ordered. Instead of killing Trinity, they decided to have a little fun first. They decided to rape and beat her. They would kill her later.

Bad mistake.

Cedrick had easily tucked the gun earlier that day with neither of the goons noticing. Now...

Payback time.

Cedrick slowly arose from the floor with his back to the wall and the gun pointed. His eyes were locked on the men hurting his sister. Angrily his chest began to heave back and forth underneath his shirt. He wanted blood.

Click-Clack!

The sound of the gun's slide being cocked echoed throughout the basement. Both rapists immediately looked in Cedrick's direction. With surprise written on their faces, they both said, "What the…"

Before they could finish their sentences, Cedrick squeezed off.

Crack!!!!!
Crack!!!!!
Crack!!!!!
Crack!!!!!

Both men immediately let go of Trinity and stumbled

8

backwards towards the wall as the force of each bullet carried them. Every single bullet tore through their chests as easily as paper. A moment later, both men fell to the floor. Weakened, Trinity collapsed to the floor also.

Rushing to his sister and taking her into his arms, Cedrick held her tightly. "Trinity," he said.

Looking up into her brother's eyes, Trinity said in a voice just slightly above a whisper, "They told me you were dead."

"I know. And for a long time I really was dead. I'm back now though." He hugged his sister tightly then allowed his emotions to flow.

"I missed you so much."

"I missed you, too."

Through tear-filled eyes, Cedrick untied his sister's wrists and helped her to her feet. He then took off his pajama shirt and placed it on her naked body. As he did so, one of the goons made a stirring sound signaling he was still alive. Eager to finish what he'd started, Cedrick took a step towards him.

Placing her hand against her brother's chest, Trinity said, "No."

Cedrick looked at his sister.

Neither of them said a word. Their eyes spoke volumes. Understanding what his sister's eyes expressed, understanding what she needed and yearned for at that moment, Cedrick handed Trinity the gun. Accepting it, she made her way barefooted across the floor to one of the surviving rapist. She took aim at him as he lay on his back.

Then...

Crack!!!!!

The bullet tore through the man's dick and severed it completely sending it flying across the room. With blood spewing from between his legs, he screamed and wriggled wildly in pain across the floor like a fish fresh out of water. Ignoring his suffering, she headed to the other goon and stood over his body as blood poured from each of the several holes ripped into his chest. Kneeling down beside him and seeing terror in his eyes, she shook her head. The bastard had the heart to inflict pain. He had the heart to kill. He had the heart to hurt people but he feared dying. With no remorse, Trinity pointed the gun at his face and repeated the same words to him that he had repeated to her earlier, "Open your mouth and suck it good. If you bite, I'll blow your fuckin' head off."

Unable to speak, his windpipe too clogged with blood and causing him to make gurgling sounds, the man did as he was told. He opened his mouth and allowed the gun's barrel into his mouth hoping Trinity would show mercy.

Cedrick said nothing. He only watched with absolutely no intentions of stopping Trinity. His sister deserved every bit of her revenge just like he deserved his.

"Suck muthafucka!" Trinity ordered.

The gunman sucked on the barrel hard. As he did, blood covered the barrel as more and more of the crimson liquid arose from his throat and damaged insides like lava. While he worked the barrel, his partner's screams finally ceased as he bled out and died.

Moments passed.

Pleased but not totally satisfied, Trinity finally took the gun from the bastard's mouth and stood. As his eyes stared up into hers, she aimed at his forehead. He took his blood covered hands from his bleeding chest and raised them for mercy, an act that meant nothing to Trinity.

She squeezed the trigger.

Blood splattered as Cedrick stood by.

As both goons now lay on the floor dead, their eyes staring up at the ceiling, Trinity stood with the gun at her side. She felt vindicated but only for the moment. She wouldn't feel *completely* vindicated until she looked directly into her mother's eyes and took her life, too.

Chapter-2

Both Nessa and Sidra walked out of the clinic and made their way through its courtyard. In a playground not far away the two friends sat down on a bench. Around them young children ran about laughing, playing and enjoying life without a care in the world. Nessa wanted to admire their worry free life but couldn't. She felt like she had no time. Too much was hitting her all at once. Just as quickly as she sat down, she stood and began to pace.

"You okay?" Sidra asked Nessa. "You've been acting antsy since we got here."

Nessa shook her head. She wasn't alright at all. What she'd already known had just been solidified by a doctor...

Nessa was pregnant.

"Hell no, I'm not okay. Shit, I'm fuckin' pregnant."

"Damn, bitch, ain't this what you wanted?" Sidra asked with her face twisted into a knot. "You always said you wanted to marry Luke and have the nigga's baby, right?"

"Yeah but that was then...this is now. Shit's different."

"Bitch, you trippin'. You just hit the damn lottery. You know how much money you can get up out that nigga for Child Support? You'll be in his pockets for the next eighteen years.

Shit, even if the relationship doesn't work out, you're good. You know how many bitches out here *wish* they could get a chance like that?"

"I just don't know about this."

Shaking her head, leaning back into the bench and crossing her legs, Sidra said, "Shit, bitch, you better check the expiration date on those drugs your ass must be takin' and quit playin'. It's time to cash in…get paid for life."

Nessa kept pacing. "Fuck Child Support!" she bellowed. In her mind she felt she was onto bigger and better things. Child Support was small time.

"I'd be happier than a faggot in the county jail if I was you," Sidra added.

Nessa was far from happy. In fact, she was spiteful.

Luke had violated.

He'd cheated on her.

And not only had he cheated. He did it with a fucking pale faced bitch. That shit hurt Nessa. It had hurt her to the point where she was entertaining abortion just to spite Luke. The thought of killing his baby made her feel like she would be killing a part of him.

Luke's infidelity now had Nessa feeling a certain kind of way towards men in general. From dealing with her father and several past boyfriends, she'd witnessed the lies, the late night trips to the store for a pack of cigarettes, the locked cell phones, the excuses, and so much more. She'd witnessed it all first hand, and now his betrayal fed her anger. She now had the chance to be the top dog in a game dominated by men. She was now going to get a chance to make their asses kneel.

"So what are you going to do?" Sidra asked.

Nessa's mind was on countless other things; the raid, Luke, possibly having Chetti killed, the million dollars she'd taken from Luke, meeting the connect, and so much more. Her mind was bombarded with way too much for her to be thinking about a baby right now. As she paced, she glanced out into the parking lot at the rental. In its trunk was five hundred thousand dollars. Knowing it was in there nervously added to her thoughts. She knew shit was about to get deep from here on out. With the addition of money, she was going to have to deal with cut throats, stick up kids and a lot more.

"Well?" Sidra asked again.

Nessa finally stopped pacing and looked at her friend. The creases in her forehead expressed what she was thinking about *possibly* doing...

"I think I'ma get on the table. Just need to make a decision."

With her bottom jaw dropped, Sidra said, "No, Nessa, you can't be serious. Now I done robbed niggas, shanked bitches and some more, but killing an unborn child ain't right."

"Sidra, you just don't understand. I've got some really big shit going on in my life right now. A baby would complicate it all."

"Damn, well are you going to tell Luke?"

"For now, I'm not even accepting the nigga's calls. And I haven't quite decided what I'm going to do about the baby yet. But whether I abort or not, fuck that nigga and fuck his feelings. He didn't care about mine when he stuck his dick in that white bitch so why should I care about his?"

"Yeah, I guess you got a point. Well, you know no matter what, I've got your back."

Children continued to laugh and play as Nessa glared at Sidra. For now she was the only person she could trust one hundred percent. Nessa had given her the other five hundred grand from Luke's money. She'd asked Sidra to keep it safe and not tell anyone, especially her greedy mother, Piper. Nessa knew that her mother would be pissed to know she'd put so much trust into Sidra. Since Sidra had a checkered past, Piper didn't trust her at all.

Even when it came down to going to see the doctor, Nessa knew that if Piper found out that Sidra was with her during such a trying moment, she would flip her wig. Luckily, for Nessa, Piper had been acting highly suspicious over the last three days. She barely answered Nessa's calls and always seemed to be whispering when she did answer. Something strange was going on with Piper…she just couldn't pin point it.

Nessa's phone rang. Seeing Brandon's number on the screen, she answered.

"You ready?" he asked.

"Yeah, I'm on my way."

"Alright."

The two ended the conversation.

"I've got to go, Sidra." Nessa stood from the bench and told her friend, "I've got to handle something serious."

"You need me to go?"

"Nah, I'm good. But look though. I'm working on something huge, something that's gonna make me rich...us rich. I'm gonna need your help though. In a minute I'm going to need only the people around me I can trust. Just guard that money I gave you with your life."

"You know I will." Sidra patted her heart letting Nessa know how she really felt about her. "Family isn't just being born with the same genes. You my family forever."

Nessa smiled.

"Now tell me what you got going on that's so damn important."

"I don't have time to talk about it now. But know you're a part of the plan. I'll hit you later."

The two hugged tightly.

Nessa hopped in her car and left the clinic. Still stressing about the pregnancy, she picked up Brandon who'd just left a Federal satellite office meeting with a few local cops . Seeing the stress on her face, he asked, "You okay?"

"I'm good," she lied.

"You sure?"

She nodded.

Unconvinced, he chose to leave it alone, but did ask about her father.

"I don't know," she said, impatiently as she kept looking

from the rearview mirror to the street ahead of her. With five hundred thousand in the trunk and a drug deal ahead of her, she couldn't help but feeling overwhelmed.

"Well, Nessa, he only gave you seventy-two hours to get the money. Something's gotta be done."

"Brandon, of course I know that. The shit's been on my damn mind constantly. But right now, first thing's first. I'll worry about my father after we've gotten this deal out the way."

Nessa made her way through traffic. Eventually she was making her way through the affluent Potomac area. Among Benzes, BMWs, and Jaguars she made her way through the neighborhood as Brandon gave her directions. Passing mansion after mansion, she reached a Spanish styled home and pulled up to its gate. After pressing a button on an intercom, she and Brandon waited.

"Yeah?" someone finally said.

"We're here to see Chavez," Nessa returned.

The gate opened slowly.

Nessa headed up a long weaving driveway towards the main house. As soon as she reached the bottom of its steps, she and Brandon were greeted by several men in black suits. Brandon was immediately searched as he stepped out of the car. His gun was confiscated. Both he and Nessa were then escorted into the house. Moments later, they were in the den.

"Brandon," Chavez emitted, sitting behind his desk in black dress pants, a black vest and a white button down shirt. He was handsome, half black and half Dominican; resembling more of a gentleman than a thug or drug dealer.

"Chavez," Brandon returned. "My man!"

Nessa was standing beside Brandon with a Louis Vuitton duffle bag filled with five hundred thousand of the one million dollars she'd snaked Luke for.

"So you must be Nessa," Chavez stated in his strong, Mexican accent. There was arrogance in his voice, and privilege in his demeanor.

She nodded, wondering why he didn't remember meeting

15

her once before.

He stood from his seat, made his way around the desk, took Nessa's hand into his, and softly planted a kiss on it. "A very beautiful woman."

"Thank you."

"And very competent if Luke actually trusts you to handle his affairs."

"Of course, I'm all that and more."

He headed back around his desk to his high-back chair. Sitting down, he leaned back and crossed his legs while folding his hands into his lap. Two gunmen with evil grimaces stood at the door watching both Nessa and Brandon carefully. If they didn't like even the slightest movement or look, they would kill.

"So I'm assuming that's my money in the bag?" Chavez asked Nessa.

"Five hundred thousand."

"Great." He signaled to one of the gunmen.

The goon headed over to Nessa and grabbed the bag of money. He then went back to the door and stood without even bothering to open the bag.

"You're not going to count it?" Nessa asked Chavez.

"Should I?"

"It's all there but I'm just saying…"

"No need," he told her passively. "You look like the type who values your life."

The room grew silent as the latter part of what he'd just said set in. The tone of his voice spoke volumes. No word or syllable was stressed causing every sound to be unsettling for Nessa. She understood exactly what he meant. If every penny wasn't in that bag...she'd be dead.

"So, how's life been treating you, Brandon?" Chavez asked, changing the topic of conversation.

"Can't complain."

"Every day above ground is one to be thankful for, huh?"

"Absolutely."

Chavez nodded. "My sympathies though for your family's recent misfortune."

"It's a part of the game. We'll pull through."

"I'm sure you will. I mean it's never easy having pigs come to seize shit they never worked for. It's thievery if you ask me."

Nessa watched Chavez as he spoke. She liked how smooth and articulate he enunciated his words. He had a demeanor similar to Luke's. But the Dominican addition to it made it even sexier. Oddly, she'd never been interested in pretty boy types.

"So, Luke will be straight…I presume?"

"Definitely," Brandon spoke up quickly. "Just a small amount of time in jail…that's all."

Returning his attention back to Nessa, Chavez said, "Five hundred thousand gets you thirty bricks. That discount is my gift to you…but I'm concerned."

"About what?" Nessa rattled her words softly.

"That seems like a lot of work for such a delicate woman." His eyes surveyed Nessa's curves.

"Trust me, Chavez. There's nothing delicate about me."

"So you can handle that much work?"

"And a whole lot more."

He chuckled as if unconvinced and said, "Cute. I guess with Luke's army behind you anything is possible." He then grabbed a small piece of paper and wrote something down on it. Extending it to Nessa, he said, "This is an address. When you leave here, head there immediately and wait outside in your car. Shortly after you arrive, the merchandise you purchased will be delivered to you."

Both Brandon and Nessa nodded.

Standing, Chavez made his way around the desk once again. Taking Nessa's hand and kissing it again, he told her, "Any problems, let me know."

"I will."

"Looking forward to doing business with you again."

"As am I."

17

As Nessa turned to head for the door, Chavez hesitated to let her hand go. There was a pause between them. They looked into each other's eyes, both sets showing obvious interest. Chavez then smiled and let go of Nessa's hand. Moments later, Nessa and Brandon were back outside in the rental and headed towards the far Southeast's Highland neighborhood, a far cry from the safe and privileged Spring Valley. Reaching it, the mansions they'd just left behind were now replaced with burned down buildings and vacant houses. Pulling to the curb in front of a store with the address on it that Chavez had sent them to, Nessa looked around at her surroundings. She saw young dope boys walking by staring at her as if they knew she didn't belong or as if they suspected she was a cop. Crackheads and prostitutes walked by staring also.

Brandon, who had been given back his gun after leaving the mansion, now pulled it out and kept it in close reach. He didn't trust the neighborhood or the people in it at all.

"You sure he's not playing us, Brandon?" Nessa asked.

Glancing in the overhead mirror, searching for anything he didn't like, Brandon said, "I'm sure. He's been doing business with the family too long to do some snake shit."

The two sat quiet.

Ten minutes passed.

A Black Tahoe pulled to the curb across the street. A moment later, its driver's side window rolled down. A young boy who looked to be no older than sixteen appeared sitting in the driver's seat. He was looking directly across the passing traffic at Nessa.

Seeing the boy, Nessa tapped Brandon. "Look."

Brandon was now looking across the street at the truck.

The young boy rolled up his window. Seconds later, the driver's side back door opened. Another young boy with tons of gold chains hopped out with two plain looking, large black book bags in his hand. Looking up and down the street, he jogged through the traffic towards the rental. Reaching it, he spat, "Roll the fuckin' window down, nigga."

Unsure if she should, Nessa looked at Brandon.

"Go 'head," Brandon told her.

She rolled it down.

Without another word said, the boy tossed the bags on Nessa's lap and jogged back across the street to the truck. He then hopped back inside. Seconds later, the truck sped off.

Nessa opened the bag. Just like Chavez had promised, there were thirty bricks of Cocaine inside.

"Alright, let's get out of here," Brandon said.

The rental rapidly pulled away from the curb. But Nessa was so nervous that when she pulled out, she failed to use a signal and was suddenly stopped by a cop looking to meet his quota. Walking up on the car with a vengeance, he frowned.

"Roll your window down," the cop spat, peering over his cheap looking shades. "License and registration."

Nessa's hand shook nervously as she cautiously reached for the glove compartment. She hoped a routine traffic stop wouldn't land her in prison for life. As she fumbled around her registration, she became increasingly more edgy.

"Why you so nervous, pretty young lady? You sweating like a pig."

Noticing his badge she began. "Officer Lucas, I don't know what I did to make you pull me over, but I'm sorry."

Nessa concocted a story about heading to see her terminally ill grandma in the hospital. The tale was so good and creatively crafted she began to believe it herself. While her lies rolled easily off her tongue, Brandon appeared to be in a daze and wearing a smirk.

"You're lying," the officer blasted. "I need you to step out of this car."

Bile rose up in Nessa's gut. "Step out for what?"

"Because I need to search this car," he said firmly. "Especially those nice duffle bags in the backseat."

"Officer, what did I do? Can you just write the ticket so we can go?" Nessa's voice cracked. "I mean this is harassment."

Her heart raced even more.

19

"I don't think so. The only place you're going is to the penitentiary. Riding around with drugs could get you life, Lady Heroine."

Nessa had to think quickly since Brandon had zoned out. While her chest heaved up and down, her first thought was to negotiate, offering a payoff. Then she thought of speeding off. More ideas scattered through her brain until Brandon finally spoke up.

"Lucas, that's enough," he blurted. "You did your job and watched my back like you were supposed to. Take this and go," he said, reaching over Nessa to hand the officer the stack of money.

"Nice doing business with you," Officer Lucas said, blowing kisses at Nessa. "She's hot, Brandon," he added, patting the inside of the window.

Immediately, Nessa reached over and punched Brandon in the chest. "If you wanna be a clown, join the fuckin' circus," she scolded skidding away from the curb.

Chapter-3

The garage door leading to the bottom of the county jail lifted. When it was completely raised, a white van with tinted windows exited the garage. Behind the van were two Ford Five Hundreds with tinted windows and government plates. Making their way through downtown during the wee hours of the morning, the small convoy hit the highway and within moments, began to place the Metropolitan area further and further behind them.

Inside the van staring at its inner walls, Luke sat in shackles and a jumpsuit. As he stared at nothing more than steel and chipped paint, he couldn't help but feel nervous and on guard. He'd awakened from his sleep shortly after 5 a.m by guards he'd never seen before, told to get dressed and then ushered out of the jail with no word of where he was going. The entire situation had him seriously suspecting the worse. He was being carried off to slaughter, a slaughter ordered by Chetti.

The game was full of betrayal. Luke knew that. He'd never doubted it. It was one of those parts of the game that no matter how much you wished it didn't exist, there was no way around it. He'd accepted it a long time ago. Still though, he'd wished it hadn't come at this point in time. He had enough damn problems, but knew his mother was ruthless.

"Where am I going?" Luke shouted to the guards.

No answer.

"What's going on?"

The driver looked at the passenger. Both men smiled at each other and chuckled. One then told the other, "It's amazing how they're man enough to snitch, but want to get nervous when it's time to take this ride."

"You won't get away with this!" he told them.

More chuckling.

The sliding window between them and Luke then slid shut.

Frustrated and worried, Luke thought about his mother and Darien. There was so much hatred in his heart for them. There was no doubt in his mind that Chetti had killed Trinity and Cedrick. And knowing how blindly and loyally Darien followed Chetti, Luke had no doubt that his brother was involved. He'd probably been the one who squeezed the trigger. Now they'd probably used their contacts on the inside to reach out and touch him for agreeing to testify against them.

Luke closed his eyes for what felt like hours. He could see his son's face. He could see Gavin lying in that warehouse on his back crying and begging to be put out of his misery. The memory made him bitter. It bred hatred. His son, despite his handicaps, deserved so much more than to die the way he did. Luke knew Gavin's death and the fact the he himself was the one who murdered his only son would remain on his conscience forever.

Opening his eyes and staring at the wall, Luke knew his options for getting out of this situation were limited. The Feds had frozen all his money so he couldn't offer to pay off the men who were probably about to kill him. What money he *did* have was tied up in the mall investment.

For some reason in the midst of the uncertainty, Luke thought about Nessa. He'd spoken to her a few times but nothing concrete was discussed. She'd let him know things were in motion. Once she got the work, she'd grind hard and get him out, she assured him. Luke heard her, yet wasn't convinced that Nessa had his back. It seemed as if he couldn't trust anyone but Pamela at the moment.

Luke truly felt like Pamela was in love with him. He didn't quite feel the way she did but he was pretending to and manipulating her. He knew her money and her connections could definitely come in handy. But now even all that seemed in vain. Everything was now about loyalty.

Luke was now even skeptical about Brandon. He sighed stressfully as he thought about all those things. "Fuck," he said in frustration as he felt the van make a sharp turn. From where he sat, he couldn't see much; only fog.

Luke began kicking at the back of the seat in front of him. "Hey, I gotta pee!" he shouted, realizing hours had passed.

No one answered.

"Hey! Can we talk about this? There's something good coming for you if we can work this shit out."

Everyone still remained silent as the van drove another forty-five minutes with all tongues motionless. Luke could feel his heart thumping through his jumpsuit.

Suddenly, the van slowed. It then made a turn onto what felt like cobblestone or some type of rocky road. Feeling the turn, Luke grew more nervous than before. He knew he was nearing his destination. The fear of the unknown had a grip on him. He finally realized he was stupid to think Chetti couldn't reach him. He was stupid to underestimate her power.

Moments passed.

The van finally stopped.

Luke listened but couldn't hear anything outside.

Finally, the back doors opened.

"Step out," an officer ordered with his hand touching his holster.

Luke was hesitant.

"Now!"

Luke stepped out reluctantly. When he did, what he saw surprised him …

In a ponytail, jumpsuit and flip flops, Chetti didn't quite look like the Chetti she'd always prided herself on. Given the circumstances though, she looked damn good. Her jumpsuit was brand new. Her ponytail was neatly combed and she smelled of Chanel's Parfum Grand Extrait; perfume costing $4200.00 per bottle.

Knowing exactly who Chetti was, the bitches and COs in Chetti's pod knew not to fuck with her. They knew she had the power to murder any of them, their families included. Because of that, they showered her with commissary, favors, phone privileges, postage stamps and everything else that inmates valued and found importance in.

"So?" Chetti asked as she sat down in the steel chair across from her attorney. "What's the latest."

"Disheartening news," Deena Phillips, a beautiful black woman of about forty years old answered. She was wearing a navy blue Dolce & Gabbana pant suit. Her long black hair fell to her shoulders. Deena was mesmerizing.

"What?"

"Luke was transferred to another jail."

"Why?"

Deena hesitated before answering.

"Well, why?" Chetti asked again impatiently.

Deena cleared her throat then glared toward the ceiling.

"He has agreed to testify for the Feds against you and Darien."

Chetti frowned instantly. She couldn't believe her ears. Shaking her head, she said, "That's nonsense. Luke would never do no punk shit like that."

Deena opened her briefcase slowly and pulled out the paperwork. She slid it across the steel table toward Chetti telling her she needed to see it for herself. Chetti snatched up Luke's agreement to testify against her and Darien. It was all there in black and white. Reading through it and then seeing his signature, she snapped. "That ungrateful son of a goddamn bitch!" she screamed. "That muthafucka!"

"I'm sorry, Mrs. Bishop," Deena shivered. She hoped none of the officers would enter the room. Chetti's voice had turned extremely loud and disturbing.

"Sorry's not going to stop that bastard from testifying. Sorry's not going to stop that bastard from destroying everything I've worked so fuckin' hard for!"

"I've got more bad news," Deena stated hesitantly.

"What?"

"Brandon knew of the raid. He wasn't directly involved in the investigation but he knew *of* everything."

"You fuckin' with me, right?"

Deena shook her head. "My source in The Bureau said Brandon definitely had knowledge."

"That snake. That fucking snake! I had that bastard on a salary. I paid that muthafucka thirty thousand dollars per month. And this is how he pays me back?" Chetti stood and began to pace the floor angrily. "They're trying to take me down. Them muthafuckas tryna play me. But I'm not going down by myself. Fuck that."

"The only way to prevent that is to try and cut a deal of your own."

Growing beyond infuriated at the suggestion, Chetti yelled, "Hell no. I'm not a rat. That's not in my character. It never has been and never will be."

"There's no other way out, Mrs. Bishop."

"Yes, there is."

"And what's that?"

Chetti made her way back to the table, rested the palms of her hands flat on the table and looked Deena directly in the eyes. "I'm going to murder them."

"Mrs. Bishop…"

"I'm going to murder Luke, Brandon and even that nappy headed girlfriend of Luke's, Nessa."

Deena just simply leaned back into her chair and accepted what she'd just heard. Obviously most attorneys would
have run after hearing their client say what Chetti had just said.
Deena wasn't your ordinary attorney though. Although a beast
in the courtroom, she was just as sleazy as they came. She had
connections in the Feds and law enforcement arena; and even
connections on the streets. That's how she'd been able to supply
Chetti with the personal information she needed to have several
people associated with the family murdered over the past several
days to keep them from possibly snitching.

"I'm going to kill them all, Deena…split their fuckin'
head down to the white meat…and eat their asses for dinner. In
the meantime, you get me out of here."

"Mrs. Bishop, I don't think…"

"Goddamn it, I don't want to hear fucking excuses!"
Chetti roared, slamming a hand down on the table. "I don't give
a fuck what you have to do. Just get me out of here!"

With that said, Chetti turned, knocked on the door and
stormed out when the guard opened it.

Darien slammed the payphone into the cradle and stood
there for a moment seething in fury and hatred. He'd just gotten
the news about Luke. For a moment he couldn't believe it. He
couldn't believe that his brother would violate blood and family
honor. Now though, despite his reluctance to believe it, he had
no choice but to.

It was what it was.

Looking around at the pod, Darien saw dozens of inmates sitting at steel tables playing cards and chess. Others conversed and laughed while watching television as if being locked
up was nothing to fret over. Seeing them all sent something
coursing through Darien's veins. He couldn't control himself,
something dangerous had taken a hold of him. Unable to restrain

himself, he grabbed the phone's receiver and watched as an inmate headed by him. Without warning, Darien swung the receiver against the unsuspecting man's head and connected squarely with his temple. Blood spewed immediately and the man went down to the floor.

The pod erupted.

Men gathered around eager to see a fight.

Dazed and dripping blood to the floor, the assaulted inmate attempted to stagger to his feet. Before he could, Darien kicked him in the side of the face so hard his neck jerked.

"Damn!" someone shouted.

"Fuck that nigga up!" someone else shouted.

As the man lay sprawled out on his back, Darien stomped him directly in the mouth knocking out several teeth. He then stomped him again.

"Aww, shit!" someone gasped. "He's gonna put that nigga in a coma!"

The CO hit the panic button behind his desk. The siren sounded.

Darien jumped on the inmate and began to beat him mercilessly. He punched him in the face as hard as he could and as many times as he could. It didn't take long before his hands were covered in blood.

The door to the pod slid open. Several COs rushed into the pod and shoved their way through the cheering inmates. Reaching Darien, they pulled him off of his victim who had now gone unconscious and whose face was barely recognizable.

"Get the fuck off me!" Darien demanded as he fought and kicked to break loose from the COs' grip.

The other inmates continued to cheer.

Darien eventually found himself lying on his stomach. His hands were then forced behind his back and handcuffed. Minutes later, he was taken to solitary, un-cuffed and shoved into an empty cell. Still pissed off at the news about Luke, he began to pace the cell wanting so badly to be free. He needed retribution. He needed revenge. He needed it all and it was destroying him inside to be deprived of it.

An hour passed.

Two passed.

Darien finally stopped pacing. Placing his hands against the wall and dropping his head, he was still angry. His adrenalin was still pumping. He didn't know what to do with any of it though. He didn't know what to do with *himself*. He'd never been in this position before. He'd never been locked up.

"Fuck!" Darien shouted banging a fist against the wall.

Darien had no idea where to go from here. Both Luke and his mother had always been the brains. They'd always been what he fed off of. Now with Luke snitching and Chetti unable to be contacted, Darien felt lost. He felt alone. But most importantly, for the very first time in his life...

He felt useless.

Chapter-4

The Ritz Carlton suite sat on the 30th floor. Stars glimmered from the night sky outside its picture windows like countless diamonds. A full moon emitted rays of white light. A breath taking view of the Crystal City skyline sat beneath the sky and stars. Along route one, the glow of cars' headlights and taillights flowed in both directions. In the bedroom scattered about were bags filled with Gucci, Dolce & Gabanna, Chanel, and a number of other fashion designers. On the dresser and nearby table were empty bottles of Ciroc and half eaten plates of Chinese food along with several stacks of money which amounted to a little over twenty thousand dollars.

Nessa was lying in the king-sized bed recuperating from a two hour long fuck fest with Brandon. Lying naked, although pregnant, her body was still shapely, no stretch marks, no outward signs of pregnancy. Her feet and hands were freshly painted and her hair was tied back. The newest Chanel perfume radiated from her pours saturating the sheets with its pleasant scent.

Lighting a cigar and laying naked himself, Brandon laid the back of his head on the stacks of pillows and stared up at the ceiling. Taking a puff of the Cohiba, savoring its taste for a moment and then exhaling, he got up, grabbed his pants and reached into his pockets. Pulling out a small baggie of cocaine, he poured the powder out on a table, positioned it into three thin lines and then pulled out a five dollar bill which he rolled up thinly. Moments later he was inhaling the Coke through the bill. As he did, Nessa watched in silence. She hadn't known he had the habit until recently.

"So how much do you know about your boy?" Brandon asked now wiping cocaine from his nostrils and looking at Nessa with his eyes growing glossy.

"Who?" she asked.

"NaNa."

"What do you mean?"

"I mean how much do you know about him?"

"Shit, everything. Why?"

Nessa thought about how far her relationship with NaNa went back. She trusted him with her life. Besides he'd proven his loyalty to her many times before.

"Are you sure he can be trusted?"

"Brandon, that's my homeboy. He's like a brother to me. I've known him since we were kids…trust the nigga with my life."

"Nessa, I'm just saying that's a lot of work you left with him to cook up."

"And?"

With more skepticism than before, he said, "I'm just say-ing."

"Brandon, don't worry about that. He's good. There's no way I would've given him that much work if he couldn't handle it."

Brandon wasn't quite assured. "How's he doing so far?"

"That shit's selling like crack in the 80's already."

"Oh, and what about Luke?"

"What about him?"

"Has he called?"

"Of course."

"What'd you tell him?"

"That I'm getting the money together."

"That's it?"

"Yes."

"Are you sure?"

"Yes, I'm sure."

"Have you told anyone else about the money and drugs."

"No, just NaNa and Sidra."

"Are you sure?"

"Are you sure Sidra can be trusted? Maybe I should hold onto that five hundred that's left. Where'd you stash it?"

"Look, Brandon, what's with the million and one questions?"

"I've got to know everything. This is real big. Can't be any slip-ups. Folks get robbed or killed in situations like this one if they're not careful."

"And you think I don't know that?"

"I didn't say you didn't. I'm just being cautious."

Nessa could feel a headache coming on. Beginning to grow annoyed, she said, "There's nothing slow about me. In case you've forgotten, my father raised me on this shit."

"I know but…"

"There are no fuckin' buts, Brandon. I know how damn serious this situation is. I know what I have to do and who I have to watch. I don't need you to hold my fuckin' hand."

With that said she slid out of bed and headed across the room to the window angrily. She gave Brandon another reason to get hard again as he surveyed her plump ass. Looking down at the street, her headache began to grow worse. Over the past few days the headaches would come and go along with emotional mood swings.

Walking over to Nessa, Brandon said, "Nessa, I wasn't trying to imply you don't know what you're doing. I just need to be sure we're on the same page." He placed a hand on her shoulder. "Where's the five hundred?"

Snatching away, she said, "Just don't touch me right now."

"Why?"

31

"Because I don't like the way you just came at me."

"What, you don't think it's fair that your partner in this thing should know everything that's going on at all times?"

"Fair has nothing to do with it. You came at me like I was a kid or something."

"Nessa, c'mon baby."

"Do you think I'm lying to you? Do you think I'm going to turn on you or something? Do you think I'm going to do something sneaky with the five hundred thousand?"

"No, of course not."

"Then stop asking me all these fuckin' questions. I know my damn position. You just focus on playing yours."

Nessa was stressed. Obviously she had a whole lot on her plate. Now along with all those things, the pregnancy was making her very emotional. It was causing her to snap uncontrollably just like right now.

Nessa's phone rang.

Both Brandon and Nessa looked at it recognizing the ring tone. It belonged to Nessa's father, Byron.

Pausing before answering, Nessa stressfully ran her hand through her hair.

"Want me to answer?" Brandon asked.

"No."

"You sure?"

"I said no, didn't I?" she snapped.

He threw his hands up in defeat.

Seconds passed.

The phone continued ringing.

Nessa finally answered.

"Your seventy-two hours are up," Byron said. "Where's my money?"

Brandon shook his head. He then headed back to the table, snorted another line of Coke and folded his arms across his chest as he stared at Nessa. He could hear Byron's voice through the phone due to the loud volume.

"Byron, I'm getting the money together right now.

You've got to understand that getting two hundred fifty thousand dollars together this quickly is next to impossible. It takes time."

"Damn that!" he yelled. "I've been giving yo' ass too much time. You're always asking for more time. I'm sick of it. You sound like a damn broken record. You think I don't know when I'm getting the fuckin' runaround?"

"I'm not giving you the runaround."

"You must really want me to give the cops this video, huh?"

"Of course not."

"Evidently you do."

"How can you be so damned cold, huh? How can you be so heartless? I'm your daughter."

"This is a cold world, Baby Girl."

Hearing him call her Baby Girl made her close her eyes tightly and cringe. She could remember how proud she felt each time he called her that as a child. Now it made her nauseous.

"A cold, *cold* world," he continued. "A dog eat dog one, too. If yo' ass have only learned only one thing in life from me, it should've been that."

Nessa wasn't surprised by his selfishness. It wasn't anything new. What had her heart enveloped in a little bit of sadness was the fact she was pregnant with Byron's grandchild. And she knew that even if she were to tell him, he'd still be just as cruel and evil. It would make no difference. The realization hurt her because it enforced the fact that she truly didn't have anyone. Pretty much everyone in her life at the moment was only there because they wanted something from her. It tugged at her heart but she refused to cry.

Brandon was still watching and listening.

"Now I'm done playin' wit' yo' ass, Nessa. I want my money by twelve thirty tonight. If I don't get it, get ready for prison life, bitch."

The phone went dead.

Gripping the phone angrily, Nessa wanted to sling it

against a wall. She wanted to spaz out. She wanted to hurt her father.

Seeing Nessa's pain, Brandon once again tried to take her in his arms.

"No!" Nessa yelled, snatching away again. Although she was hurting, she had to watch how and who she showed her emotions to; it was something her father taught her.

"Nessa, two hundred fifty thousand is going to leave us with only half of the five hundred thousand," Brandon told her.

"Do you think I'm retarded? I know that. I can count."

"And even if you give it to him, he'll never be satisfied. He'll just keep on coming back for more. That's the way guys like him are. I've seen it countless times. They bleed people dry."

Nessa rubbed her hand through her hair nervously. "Mo' money, mo' problems," she whispered to herself.

"So, what do you want to do?"

"We've got to set him up somehow like we intended to do in the first place."

"How, Nessa? You said yourself he taught you about this life. I highly doubt he'll be easy to set up."

Nessa knew he was right.

"Nessa, there's only one option."

"What?"

"We kill him."

"No."

"Nessa, why not?"

"No, I said."

"Nessa, it's the only way."

"Brandon, what part of the damn word *no* do you not understand? I said *no*."

Nessa wanted her father dealt with. She wanted him punished. She wanted revenge but she couldn't bring herself to kill him. She didn't love him a whole lot but there was love there. Although only a morsel, it was there none the less. And it wouldn't allow her to be as cruel to him as he was being to her.

34

Shaking his head, Brandon asked, "Well, what do you suggest? What do you want to do? Obviously you don't have two hundred fifty thousand for him right now."

Beginning to pace the floor, Nessa thought. Several moments later, she said, "Fuck it. We're going to meet him at twelve thirty."

"But you don't have the money."

"I know. He doesn't know that though. When we get there, we're going to kidnap him."

"Then what?"

"We'll hold him until I can figure out what to do next. Maybe we can beat some sense into him. Maybe get him to leave town."

That was music to Brandon's ears. Besides killing Byron, he could think of nothing more he wanted to do to him than breaking a couple bones.

Nessa put on her robe and grabbed her phone. She dialed Piper's number again for the fifth time within the last couple of hours. All of her calls had been sent straight to voice mail. The fact that her mother wasn't answering her calls was beginning to worry her. Had Piper's years of deceitfulness caught up with her?

"Who are you calling?" Brandon asked.

Nessa shot him a crazy look. She didn't want Brandon thinking he had any control over her.

"I asked you a question," he stated wildly.

"And I ignored you, didn't I?" she said, setting the phone down.

"Look Nessa, I don't know what's gotten into you, but we've got another problem," Brandon told her.

"What problem?"

"The guys who shot up Gavin's funeral. Londo's crew."

"What about them?"

"The deal you and I made them. They still expect us to come through on it."

Looking at him like he'd gone crazy, she asked, "The

35

deal *you* and *I* made them? I didn't make a deal with them. *You* made a deal with them."

"Where's the other five hundred thousand?"

"In safe keeping."

"I'm serious, Nessa. These guys aren't to be played with. Where's the five hundred thousand?"

"I told you it's in safe keeping."

Nessa didn't like where this was going. She definitely didn't like being included in Brandon's bullshit. "Why do you want to know where it is? You've asked me that question a million damn times."

"Because I told them you would pay them off until I can make good on the deal."

"*Me*?!" she screamed.

"Shit, you're the one with the money. You're the one taking over the family."

"Brandon, what the fuck?"

Grabbing her by the arms, he said assuring her, "Just fifty thousand, Nessa. That's all. That's all we need to keep them off our asses."

Pissed, Nessa said, "I can't believe you. You put me in your damn mess?"

"Nessa, I had to. They would've killed me if I didn't have anything to offer."

"So, to take the heat off *your* ass, you decided to put it on *mine*?"

"Relax."

"Fuck that!"

Nessa was seeing red. She felt like she was being pimped and played.

"Don't worry," he told her as he turned to get dressed. "Just get the fifty thousand and everything will be cool."

Eyeing him, he no longer looked sexy or attractive to Nessa. He looked like a snake, a snake whom she definitely wasn't going to let know where the remaining five hundred thousand dollars was, and a snake she would be watching very closely from here on out.

"I've got to go make a quick run," he said after getting dressed.

"Where you going?"

"Gotta do something real quick. I'll be back by twelve so we can meet your father." He kissed her on the cheek and headed for the door.

As Nessa watched Brandon leave, she had an uneasy feeling about him, a feeling she'd never had about him until tonight. To put it plain and simple...

She didn't trust him. Fucking cokehead.

The interior of the car was dark and silent. No music played from the radio. No conversation between the inhabitants. Everything and everyone was totally still as two cigarettes were puffed on and passed, their smoke filling the car.

Across the street the brightly lit entrance of the Ritz Carlton was in clear sight. Staring across passing traffic, the men in the car had been parked at the curb for the past few hours watching the entrance like a hawk. None of them had gotten out to even piss or stretch their legs. They wanted to be ready to move as soon as Brandon's face appeared.

Finally, Brandon walked out..

Each man in the car arose in their seats, their eyes locked on Brandon.

Brandon jogged across the street to his car oblivious to the fact he was being watched. Slipping into the driver's seat and pulling out into traffic, he headed up the street. As he did, the car he was being watched from pulled into traffic also. Inside it...guns were being cocked.

Filthy Rich-2 BY: KENDALL BANKS

Chapter-5

It still seemed like a dream.

His voice.

His touch.

His smell.

It had all been taken away from Trinity for so long that none of it seemed real to her even though she could physically reach out and touch her brother. She felt like it would all be cruelly snatched away from her once again. If it did, she couldn't take it. She couldn't take finally having her brother back and then losing him again. It would kill her. That was why she was vowing to never let that happen again. She'd kill Chetti, Luke and Darien in cold blood before she would allow that to happen again.

Both Trinity and Cedrick were sitting in the living room of one of Trinity's closest friend's home, Amelia. She and Trinity had been close since they were in kindergarten. These days she was the only person Trinity trusted. She'd also had a crush on Cedrick during her childhood years but was too young to act on it.

After doing a little shopping, Amelia now walked in the door with bags from Payless and Walmart. They were filled with clothes. Not the type of fashion brands Trinity was used to but they were clothes nonetheless.

"Got everything you needed," Amelia said.

"Thanks," both Trinity and Cedrick said in almost unison.

Neither Cedrick nor Trinity had a penny to their name. They had no clothes or any belongings. Trinity didn't even have an ID or Social Security card. Without those things, she couldn't go to the bank to get money out of her account. Since the Feds had seized the mansion and two police cars were now sitting outside the home, twenty-four seven, they couldn't get inside to get anything. So since they couldn't, Amelia was cool enough to get some things for them she could afford out of her own pocket.

Amelia was the nerdy type, always dressed in loose clothing, shabby shoes, and one who never quite went out much and didn't have too many friends. She was built sloppily. She wore glasses. She hadn't had too many boyfriends in her life. But for what she lacked in looks, she more than made up for in heart and consideration. She was a very nice person who would give you the shirt off her back when you needed it.

"You guys hungry?" Amelia asked. Before they could answer, she said, "Let me go fix you something anyway."

"We don't want to be a bother," Cedrick said. He thought about how they had to use a stranger's phone on the side of the road to even call Amelia.

"Nonsense," she said. "I got you."

"You sure?" Trinity asked.

"Don't worry. You know I rarely get company. So when I do, it's an honor for me to entertain. And you need to put those ice packs back on your face, Missy."

Standing up from the couch, Trinity hugged her friend and said, "As soon as I get straight, I'm going to pay you back."

Amelia stared at all the bruises on her friends face and body. "Don't worry, girl. No payback needed."

Amelia headed to the kitchen. But just before she did, she smiled at Cedrick real sexy-like to let him know she still had

40

that same crush on him since a little girl. Even his scruffy afro and beard couldn't stop her from liking him.

Now alone, both Cedrick and Trinity stressed over their current situation again.

"Just when I thought Chetti couldn't surprise me with her bullshit, she does," Trinity said. Shaking her head, she leaned back into the couch and asked, "How do you give the order to have your own daughter murdered? How could she?"

Tears welled up in her eyes, yet she refused to let them fall.

Cedrick was hurting for his battered sister much more than he was hurting for himself. "I wish I knew, Trinity."

"It's like God cursed us. He gave everyone else normal parents but chose to give *us* the fucked up ones." Bitterness, pain and sadness were evident in Trinity's tone.

Cedrick placed a hand on his sister's shoulder to console her. She shrieked from the pain.

"Rape, molestation, abuse," she said with tears continuing to form. Shaking her head, she continued, "No matter how hard I try, I can't get the smell of dad's after shave out of my head. I can still remember its smell as he was molesting me."

Cedrick cringed at his sister's words. He took her carefully in his arms and let her rest the side of her face against his chest. He wanted to protect her.

"That shit'll never leave me," she told him. "I still remember getting pregnant by the boy next door and mom having that damn doctor come over to make me abort the child while forcing me to have Luke's later on." Tears fell from her eyes. "I hate them. I hate them with a passion."

"I know exactly how you feel," Cedrick said. "You're not by yourself in this. I knew Chetti could be an evil bitch but I had no idea she would go as far as to have me kidnapped and drugged up."

The memory of the night of Cedrick's kidnapping filled his head.

"I was in denial when it first happened. I didn't think she

could do something like that to me, her own son. I just couldn't. It didn't become clear until I actually saw her face and saw her giving orders to my kidnappers from her own damn mouth."

Trinity pulled closer to her brother. She felt just as bad for him as he did for her.

"The ultimate betrayal," he muttered.

"Yeah," she agreed. "The ultimate betrayal."

The brother and sister team sat in silence and in each other's arms for what seemed like forever. Eventually Trinity wound up falling asleep on Cedrick's chest. When she did, he softly slid out from underneath her head careful not to wake her. Grabbing one of the Walmart bags, he pulled out an outfit and a pair of new clippers. He then headed up the stairs to the bathroom and shut the door. Moments later, when he emerged, he didn't look anything like he did when he first went in. In new clothes, his beard and afro was now gone. His walk more confident. His demeanor seemed more sophisticated.

As Cedrick made his way back down the stairs, Trinity awoke from her sleep at the same time that Amelia was bringing the food she'd cooked into the living room. Both women laid eyes on Cedrick at the very same moment. Neither woman could believe how different he looked. Trinity herself had almost forgotten how handsome her brother was just before the kidnapping. Women swooned over him even more than they did Luke.

Trinity had to check her feelings. Strangely, her insides yearned for her brother. She snapped out of it quickly, before Cedrick hit the bottom of the stairs.

I refuse to let my mother's and father's spirit get inside of me, she told herself.

"Sorry, Amelia, but I'm going to have to eat later." He smiled widely toward Amelia's growing grin. "Just take good care of Trinity for me while I'm gone. And when I get back we're going to the hospital to report a rape and get you checked out."

Trinity frowned showing her disapproval.

"We must," he said firmly. "Those guys could have all

kinds of diseases. So be ready when I get back."

"Okay…But where are you going?" Trinity asked.

"I need to go see Mr. Falou."

"Dad's old attorney?"

"Yes."

"Why?"

"He set up my inheritance when dad died. I have to go see where it stands."

Trinity shook her head up and down repeatedly. Her facial expression showed that she totally agreed.

"Chetti's a slick bitch," Cedrick added. "Those prison walls won't hold her ass for too long. She'll find a way out. And she'll be looking for us the moment she finds out we're alive."

Filthy Rich-2 BY: KENDALL BANKS

Chapter-6

The prison was located in a small town near the outskirts of Fredericksburg, Maryland. And although surrounded with fences and barbwire, it didn't have the menacing look and atmosphere of other prisons. In fact, it simply looked like a gathering of cottages, each surrounded by newly manicured green lawns.

Luke was sitting in his air conditioned one-man cell watching television; a luxury he didn't have back in the county jail. He was wearing a new white Nike track suit and a pair of Air Force 1 kicks… instead of a state issued jumpsuit. On his wrist was a platinum Rolex. In his foot locker were several more folded brand new sweat suits. On a nearby shelf sat numerous books along with several hundred dollars worth of commissary. From the window was a view of the compound with nearby woods sitting off in the distance.

Still kept in protective custody and unable to mingle with the other prisoners, Luke was able to move around a lot more in the prison camp than he was in his previous location. Here he had a job in the kitchen, was able to walk the yard alone for two hours per day and was able to work out in a state of the art gym. He was also given better access to the phones. It was obvious that not only were the Feds taking care of him, someone's money was taking care of him also.

That someone?

Pamela.

Luke was thankful to find out upon his arrival that Chetti was not responsible for his move. A sigh of relief filled him days ago when he realized the prosecutors had set up his transfer to keep him safe until time to testify.

"Mr. Bishop?" a voice came over the cell's intercom.

"Yeah," Luke answered.

"You've got a visit."

"Alright."

Luke got off his bunk, brushed his teeth and ran a brush over his freshly low cut Caesar. He then looked at himself in the mirror. He definitely looked more like the Luke he'd been when free. Satisfied, he put on cologne. A moment later, his cell door was opened. He was then escorted out of his dorm. Minutes later, he and the officer were approaching a row of white trailers, each furnished and designated for conjugal visits; a privilege only given to special inmates.

"Two hours, Mr. Bishop," the guard said.

Nodding, Luke opened the door of the trailer and walked inside to see Pamela sitting on the couch. He smiled.

"Hey, baby," Luke said as he headed towards Pamela. "I knew it was you who pulled all of this off for me." Luke quickly thought back to his initial ride to his new home at Bernwood Correctional Facility. He could now find humor in how he thought he was being led to his death but instead a place where he could have more freedom.

"You look so damnnnnn good," he hissed, feeling overly horny.

Pamela Benson was dressed in a white Valentino blouse and a black pencil skirt showing off her flat stomach and flat ass. On her feet were a pair of Christian Dior sandals. Standing and accepting Luke into her arms, Pamela rested the side of her face against Luke's chest.

Luke took in the scent of Pamela's body and perfume.

The scent of women had never been a big deal to him when he was free. These days, the scent of a woman was priceless to him. There was nothing in the entire universe like it. Pamela's scent was immediately beginning to make Luke hard. With his dick bulging in his sweats, he began to kiss Pamela around her neck. He needed her. He needed her badly.

"Luke," she said, while stepping back from him. "Luke, I have something to tell you."

"It can't wait?" He was horny beyond measure.

Pamela looked at him silently and with a sort of sadness written on her face, a look Luke had never seen on her before. "What's wrong?" he asked.

"It's bad. You should sit down."

"I prefer to stand. What is it?"

Pamela froze for what seemed like forever. Her face became flushed with sorrow.

"What is it?" Luke asked worriedly. "Has someone done something to you?"

Pamela shook her head…then buried her head into his chest.

"Tell me, Pamela. What is it?"

"Your brother."

"Darien?"

She nodded.

"What about him?"

She grew uneasy about speaking further. She knew what she was about to tell him would tear him apart.

"Well?" he asked. "What about him?"

After pausing several moments more, she said, "He's dead."

Although delivered softly, those two words slammed into Luke like a truck. "What do you mean?"

She couldn't bear to say anymore. She hesitated.

Stepping a few steps away from Pamela, Luke demanded, "What do you mean? What are you saying?"

"I don't know everything. I only know what I've heard.

From what I've been told, they found his body beaten and bloody in his cell. I think he was stabbed multiple times."

The images flashed in Luke's mind of his brother's dead body. They made him cringe.

"An investigation has been opened. They're not sure if the jail was involved or if the murder was committed by an inmate."

Luke's knees almost gave out. He sat down on the arm of the couch and dropped his eyes to the floor in disbelief. He couldn't believe his brother was gone.

"I'm sorry," Pamela said softly. She ached for him. The last thing she wanted was to see him hurting.

A tear fell from Luke's eyes and rolled down his cheek.

"Baby," Pamela said, placing a hand on his shoulder.

Snatching away, Luke wiped the tear from his eyes, stood from the couch and headed to the far side of the room. Sadness for his brother turned into uncertainty. He had to remember that his brother wasn't an angel. His brother wasn't innocent. The realization of those things countered the sadness. As badly as he wanted to cry, he wanted his brother to burn in hell. The problem was he didn't quite know which feeling should win.

Pamela stared at Luke's back.

Luke began to see his mother's face in his mind. He wondered if she'd heard about Darien's death. Although he hated her, he knew this would both be a tough time for her, and that retaliation would begin.

Pamela slowly walked towards Luke again. Reaching him, she placed her arms around him. She wanted so badly to console him. Luke turned around and wrapped his arms around her. He then began to kiss her but with a more intense feeling than ever before. With anger and sadness flowing through him, he reached behind her head, snatched a hold of her ponytail, jerked her head back and began to kiss her around the neck. He then forcefully backed her against a wall while continuing to kiss her neck.

48

"Ohhhhhhhh, Luke," she moaned.

Luke snatched Pamela's skirt up to reveal the fact that she wasn't wearing any panties. Now kissing her in the mouth and tasting her tongue, he lifted one of her legs to expose her cleanly shaven pussy.

"Luke," she moaned again.

Pulling down his sweat pants and exposing his erection, Luke forced himself into Pamela so hard she winced in pain. Taking it, she bit into his shoulder to muffle a scream. She then grabbed hold of his body and dug her nails into his chocolate skin.

Chetti and Darien's faces flashed in Luke's head. Seeing them, he began to drill Pamela like a beast. He began to use his dick like a weapon. Angrily, he pounded in and out of her as hard as he could, purposely wanting to hurt her.

"Luke!" Pamela screamed in both pain and pleasure.

He continued going deep. He continued inflicting punishment. As he did, Chetti and Darien continued to appear in his head. The more they did, the more he dug harder, the deeper he went.

"Luke, oh God!" She screamed at the top of her lungs. She'd never in her life been fucked as hard as she was being fucked right now. It hurt so badly but she refused to beg for her mercy. She knew Luke needed to release frustration. She knew he needed to let out his anger at what she'd just told him. So as his woman, she felt it was her responsibility to take the punishment he inflicted between her vanilla thighs.

Luke pounded and drilled for nearly fifteen minutes before he finally exploded. After he did, he and Pamela continued to hold each other as they slid down the wall and sat on the floor recuperating. Silence fell between them. Their breathing was heavy at first. It slowed as time passed. So did their heartbeats.

"You okay?" Pamela finally asked.

He nodded.

"You sure?"

"I'll make it."

49

She nestled as deeply into his arms as she could. "How you been holding up in here?"

"It's better than the county."

"Need anything?"

"I'm fine. You've done enough."

Pamela had paid for Luke's clothes, television, and had placed money on his books. Through family connections, she'd been able to get the prison to allow conjugal visits and other privileges.

"Thanks for everything," he told her.

"Don't worry about it."

"How's the 5 Points deal?"

She sighed. "Baby, I'm stalling the other current investors as long as I can. Other investors want in. I'll keep stalling but I can't guarantee it'll be for too much longer. My father is one of the current investors. Right now he's got a few other things on his plate that are keeping him preoccupied. But once those things are handled, which won't be too long from now, he's going to be focused on 5 Points. Once that happens…"

Luke sighed. He knew what Pamela was getting at. He wanted the 5 Points deal badly. With the money it would bring in, obviously he'd be set for life. He definitely didn't want to lose out on the chance.

"I appreciate you," he told her. "My lawyer's working hard to get my accounts unfrozen. As soon as he does, I'll get my end to you."

"I know," she said sweetly.

The two sat in silence.

Finally, she asked, "Are you having any second thoughts about testifying against your mother?"

Shaking his head, he answered, "No."

"Wow."

"Why do you say that?"

"I'm trying to picture myself testifying against my dad."

"Your dad isn't my mother. My mother has hurt a lot of

people. She's the most selfish and coldhearted person I know. Loyalty and family mean nothing to her."

Luke hadn't gone into exact detail with Pamela about the case. He'd simply told her he had made mistakes and had lived a life on the other side of the law. But he'd changed. He wanted out of that life. That was why he had come to her to invest in the 5 Points deal.

"My family is so close knit," she continued. "It would kill me to have to be in your position."

"Family can sometimes be your worst enemy."

"Still, sitting in that courtroom looking at her face has to unnerve you a little."

With flashes of the faces of countless men he'd killed darting through his mind, he said, "I've seen worse."

The two continued to hold each other. Neither said a word. Their embrace was all that needed to be spoken. As they held each other, Luke's mind couldn't help but drift to Nessa. It had been two weeks since he'd heard from her. And now she wasn't accepting his calls. He also hadn't been able to reach his connect, Chavez to see if she'd been in contact with him. Shaking his head, Luke was starting to believe Nessa had taken the money and run. He wondered what she was doing at that moment with his money and who she was with.

As if sensing what Luke was thinking, Pamela asked in almost a whisper, "Have you dumped Nessa?"

Without hesitation, he answered, "Yes. I told you I would."

As they continued to sit in silence, although Luke was sure he was done with Nessa, he was still yearning to see her one last time. But not to kiss her. Not to make love to her. No, what he wanted was much more intimate. He wanted to see her one final time so he could look into her eyes as he killed her.

In an examination room in Johns Hopkins Cardiology Center, Piper sat on the bed in only an examination apron and socks. The doctor was standing next to the bed holding her latest X-rays and test results. "So?" Piper asked.

Sighing and then looking at Piper with regret, he answered, "I'm sorry, Ms. Kingston. As expected, the cancer is spreading to your chest."

Piper dropped her eyes to the floor. Those words hurt. Even the fact that she was expecting them didn't help to ease their effect. They still left her almost breathless.

Piper's days on earth were now truly numbered.

"I'm sorry," the doctor said.

Piper had been diagnosed with Stage 3 Lung cancer over a month ago. She hadn't been feeling well over the last few weeks but managed to live decently until now. She'd now been coughing a lot and extremely weak. She didn't have an appetite. And when she did eat, her stomach wouldn't hold it down. The lack of eating was causing her to lose weight. Finally, accepting the fact that she had no other choice but to go visit a doctor, she finally went. That was when the news was broken to her.

"How long do I have left?" she now asked.

"A few months."

Chills ran down her spine. She was coming to grips with her mortality. It was a terrifying feeling. There was so much dirt she'd done in her life...she didn't believe she would be given mercy. She began asking all sorts of questions. "You think I'll start coughing up blood? And what about my time," she belted with concern. "You sure I only have a few months?"

"Piper, let's take this one step at a time."

"Doc, pleaseeeeee, I don't know what else to do."

Piper conversed for several more moments with the kind doctor before his departing.

Hesitating before getting dressed, Piper stood from the bed and headed to the window. Looking out at passing traffic, she got lost in thought and memories. As she watched everyone go about their business and lives, she wished she could be one of them. She wished she had made better decisions in life. She wished she had achieved more. But now accepting that things couldn't be changed, she got dressed and headed out of the room. On the elevator she began coughing heavily. Her coughs were hard, gravelly sounding. But despite the coughing, as she traveled down to the first floor on the elevator, her body was anticipating one thing, the one thing that had gotten her in this mess in the first place...

A damn cigarette.

Now outside, Piper went in her purse, pulled out a pack of cigarettes, and lit up. Feeling the smoke in her infected lungs, she felt relief despite how cursed and how momentarily. She then called Nessa. They had not spoken regularly and she debated on telling Nessa about her prognosis.

Piper hadn't told Nessa about the cancer. She hadn't mentioned it to her daughter at all. She hadn't even given hint of it in her appearance. She continued to keep her hair done, her face beat and her clothes crispy. She refused to let anyone know she was hurting and near death.

"Yeah?" Nessa answered.

"Where you at?" Piper snapped.

"Handling business. But the real question is, where have you been, Ma? I've been calling you for days."

"Been busy."

"Busy?? First, you hunt me down like prey, watching my every move...then you disappear and I can't get in contact with you."

"Look, you get money from NaNa yet?"

"It's coming slow."

"What do you mean?"

"I mean word has gotten around to everyone Luke did business with that the family's locked up. They're all scared the Feds are watching. Not too many of them want to do business with us."

Growing angry, Piper said, "Nessa, I don't want to hear excuses. Make shit happen."

"What the hell do you think I've been trying to do? It's going to take time."

Obviously time was a gift Piper didn't have too much of.

"Look, I need money, and I need it sooner than later."

"Just hold tight , Ma. I've been dealing with a lot."

"And. What the fuck are you expecting…a violin to play? Or what you want a hug? Bitch please, this grown folks shit right here. Handle it."

"I'm trying. And this fuckin' Brandon is a damn Coke head?"

"What?"

"Yes, he's a damn Coke head?"

"What do you mean?"

"I mean he's snorting Cocaine like fifty going north. Every time I look around, he's got his nose buried in the shit. And he's supposed to be guiding me in this shit."

Piper had no idea Brandon was using cocaine.

"And he's got me tied up in some shit with these crazy Cholos out of Los Angeles."

"Is it serious?"

"Not yet. Nothing a little money can't buy me out of. But still, I don't like being surprised."

Piper felt her daughter. When folks got caught up in snorting Coke, they didn't think straight. They got sloppy.

"I'm starting to feel like he can't be trusted," Nessa said.

"Well, just keep an eye on him for now."

"Alright."

Piper was getting ready to hang up.

"Mom?"

"Yeah?"

"Looking back on when you and dad were together, did you ever want him dead?"

"Why would you ask that?" The question caught Piper off guard.

"Just curious."

Piper thought back on her relationship with Byron. It was

rough at times; actually most times. When it was good it was good, but then when it was bad it was dreadful.

"Well, did you?" Nessa asked again.

"No."

Silence.

"Why did you ask that?" Piper asked.

Silence.

Then...

"No reason," Nessa answered.

The line then went dead.

Holding the phone in her hand, Piper stood there not liking the tone of that conversation. Something wasn't right. Whatever it was, she had a feeling it would affect things from here on out.

Chapter-7

Nessa pulled up to NaNa's and climbed out of the car. Heading up the walkway towards the porch, her mind was still being pulled in numerous directions. She'd never been this restless before in her entire life. At the moment, the one thing that was stressing her out the most was her father. Damn, why did he have to be such a fucking asshole? Why couldn't he be a damn father? Shaking her head, Nessa could only accept that her father was as deadbeat as they came. Hopefully, what she had planned for him later would knock some sense into his head.

Reaching the door, Nessa knocked. As she did, she looked around at the dark street. Slipping her hand into her purse, she rested its palm on the handle of a gun. She didn't trust the streets. She knew far too well that they could reach out and touch her at any time, simply out of jealousy and envy. She'd be damned if she was going to get caught slipping.

After peeking out of the curtain, which was a bed sheet nailed over the window, NaNa opened the door with a gun in his hand. Like Nessa, he didn't trust the streets either.

"What up, Nessa?" he asked shirtless and dressed in a pair of Dickies and Jordan's.

"Came to pick that up," she said, looking at the way he was dressed. She always felt like NaNa needed to dress more like his age. At forty-one he wasn't getting any younger.

"Cool."

After closing the door and tucking the gun in his pants, NaNa grabbed a blunt from the cocktail table and took a pull. After offering Nessa a hit, which she declined, he led her through the house to the kitchen.

"Shit's definitely been picking up lately. The work is moving like crazy. Muthafuckas been blowin' my damn phone up for the past couple days."

Those words were music to Nessa's ears.

"That's what I wanna hear!"

Reaching the kitchen, NaNa opened a cabinet and pulled out ten boxes of Pops cereal. Opening them, he then pulled out stacks of money. "A little over four hundred thousand," he said. "I did what we planned to triple the profit."

Nodding approvingly, Nessa loved how the money felt in her hand. "Good job. Any problems?" she asked.

"Nahhh, shit been good so far. But I'm keepin' my eyes and ears open. You know how it is out here. Muthafuckas see you makin' major moves, and word spreads. Niggas start gettin' jealous."

"Well, don't stunt. That shit draws too much attention."

"Don't worry."

"And of course you got somebody reliable running the other house, right?"

"Hell yeah. My system is the shit…they cook & move baby, before anybody can blink."

"Bet. And your team; are they keeping their mouths shut?"

"Yeah, they know. I don't play that shit. We all know I'm the master at this game."

NaNa had recruited some of his seasoned workers that he trusted with his life to help move the work. For him, the entire process had been successful thus far.

"Anyway, the way this work is starting to move, you're going to have to re-up soon. I definitely think we'll have the last of this coke moved by the end of the week."

"I got you."

Getting the money was the best news Nessa had received since deciding to cross Luke. Shit was coming together. She now knew that as long as she stayed focused with NaNa and the crew of pups he'd recruited, the sky was the limit. All she had to do was make sure NaNa was getting his twenty-five percent as promised.

After leaving NaNa and now sitting in the driver's seat of the rental again with the money in the backseat, Nessa smiled for the first time in a while. Everything had been worth it, she realized. She was coming up. And in no time, she could envision herself taking Chetti's spot. The thought made her snicker as it was accompanied by the memory of she and Chetti arguing the night Luke her set up. She remembered as she lay on that bed aching and battered, she had promised Chetti she was going to take over. She was now keeping that promise.

The cell rang.

Looking at the screen, Nessa knew who the call was from. It didn't have a name but she recognized the number. "Yeah," she answered.

"You don't know how to answer your phone these days?" Luke's voice asked. Despite his anger, he kept his tone calm.

Leaning back in the seat, truly feeling herself, Nessa said, "Been busy."

"Is that right?"

"Yup."

There was a cockiness and sarcastic tone to Nessa's voice. She laced her voice with it on purpose. She wanted Luke to hear in her tone that she no longer needed him.

"Too busy to handle the orders I gave you, huh?"

Nessa sighed loudly hoping to get as far underneath Luke's skin as possible. "Isn't it obvious?"

Luke grew silent.

"Cat got your tongue, Luke? Well, just so you know, I knew about that white bitch. Yeah, I knew about Pamela. I knew

59

you were playing me like a fool the whole damn time. That's why I took the money and left your ass in there to rot."

Luke laughed.

"What's so fuckin' funny?"

"So, you think I'm going to rot in here, huh?"

"Nigga, with all the shit the Feds got on you, they're going to put your ass *under* the jail. And while you're there, me and my child will be living beautifully off your money."

"Child?"

"Yes, Luke, I'm pregnant. And the baby is yours. But that's none of your concern. You'll never see it."

Luke couldn't keep his composure anymore. He lost it. "Listen here, you back stabbing bitch. Stealing from me was the worst mistake you could've ever made. When I get out of here; and yes, bitch, I *will* get out of here, I'm going to carve that baby out of your belly and kill both of you muthafuckas side by side. That's a promise!"

The call ended.

Chills ran down Nessa's spine. She'd never seen that side of Luke. She honestly began to wonder if he could possibly get out. If he did, she was going to make sure she had her shit tight. She would have shooters on her payroll.

Seeing that it was almost eleven thirty on the dashboard's digital clock, Nessa started up the car and headed to Sidra's. She was going to stash the money over there until she hooked up with Chavez again for a re-up. Also, with Brandon acting strange lately and snorting himself into a stupor, she didn't trust leaving that type of money around him. She didn't want him to even know how much she'd gotten from NaNa. In fact, if Brandon didn't get his act together, she was going to cut his ass off *period*.

Nessa pulled away from the curb and headed to Sidra's. She drove quickly knowing she had to meet Brandon for the meeting with Byron. Arriving at Sidra's, she grabbed the money and quickly hopped out of the car. Looking around for anything or anyone she didn't trust, Nessa made her way to the front door and knocked. Seconds later, Sidra opened the door. Quickly brushing passed her, Nessa walked into the living room and said, "I need you to hold this."

"What is it?" Sidra asked, closing the door.

"More money. Four hundred thousand, but I'ma take fifty grand with me and give you 350k. Gotta go handle something right quick."

"Alright, I got you."

Nessa handed her the bag. "I can't trust Brandon's ass. So if he comes sniffing around and asking you questions about the money, don't tell him you'vc got it."

"Why, what's wrong?"

"He's just been acting real strange lately. Plus, he's on that shit."

"Crack?"

"Coke."

"Same thing. He's a crackhead either way it goes."

"Well, whatever he is, I don't trust him. I think I might have to cut his ass loose."

"Shit, that might be best. But be careful. He's a Fed so that shit can get real tricky. You got eight hundred and fifty grand in your possession now."

"I know."

Nessa looked at hcr watch. Seeing she only had fifteen minutes to get to the meeting, she said, "I got to go. Stash that money good."

"Don't worry about it. I told you this is the safest place as long as nobody knows I got it."

"Bet."

Nessa left Sidra's, hopped back in the rental and headed for the meeting. She grew a little nervous, not quite sure how it would turn out. Arriving at the park where she and Brandon had met Byron before, Nessa saw Brandon's car parked. Hopping out of her car, she headed across the lot underneath the night's darkness and climbed in Brandon's passenger seat. "He here yet?" she asked.

Sniffing a line of cocaine from a small piece of paper, he said, "Nope."

Looking at him with disgust, she asked, "Well, damn, how would you know? You've got your face buried in that shit."

"I just needed a quick hit. It's not a problem. Don't worry."

Nessa looked at Brandon closely. He looked sweaty. His eyes were red.

"Don't look at me like that," he told her. "I told you I'm good."

She didn't believe him.

"You heard about Darien?" he asked.

"No, what about him?"

"He's dead."

"What?"

"Unbelievable, huh?"

"What happened?"

"He was found in his cell fucked up pretty badly... Stabbed up so I heard"

"Who did it?"

"Don't know yet. All I do know is Chetti is on a rampage right now, one worse than before. She's having people killed right and left. You definitely better watch yourself."

Pulling a gun from her purse, she said, "Trust me; I am."

"Good."

Looking around for Byron, Nessa glanced at her watch. It was eleven o'clock on the dot. "Where is he at?"

"He'll be here. Lowlifes like him can't resist the chance to fuck somebody over."

"Well, just remember we're going to try and talk some sense into him first. If that doesn't work, we're simply going to kidnap him. That's it. We're not going to kill him. I just want to scare some sense into him if worse comes to worst."

Brandon snorted another line of coke.

"Do you hear me?" Nessa asked.

"Yeah, yeah, I got you."

"And put that damn shit away."

He wrapped what was left of the cocaine back up in paper and stuffed it in his pocket.

The two sat for several moments waiting.

Then Byron appeared ahead of them. He stepped out from the darkness of the trees and made his way towards the car. Seconds later, he was sitting in the backseat. Looking behind him out the back window he asked, "Who is that?"

"Who is who?" Nessa asked.

"The muthafucka in that car parked across the street."

Nessa turned and looked out the back window while Brandon looked at his rearview. They both saw a car parked across the street but its interior was too dark to see if anyone was inside.

"Who is it?" Byron asked again.

"I don't know," Nessa told him.

"The car pulled up and parked there about twenty minutes ago. Nobody ever got out."

"Well, what does that have to do with us?"

"I don't know, bitch. You tell me."

"Watch how you speak to her," Brandon demanded.

"Fuck you."

"No, fuck *you*!"

"Calm the hell down!" Nessa yelled.

"This supposed to be some kind of okey doke?" Byron asked, pulling a .38 Revolver from underneath his shirt.

"What the fuck are you talking about? Whoever is in that car has nothing to do with us."

"For your damn sake, they better not. Now where's my Goddamn money?"

"Byron," Nessa said.

"Don't Byron me. I don't want to hear *shit* except where my fuckin' money is."

Nessa reached in her purse and pulled out fifty thousand dollars, which she had taken from the money she'd stashed at Sidra's. Turning to her father, she said, "You're a business man,

63

Byron. So I'm going to appeal to that side of you. This is fifty thousand."

"Goddamn it, I said I wanted two hundred fifty," he yelled.

"Byron, look."

"No, bitch. *You* look. I'm done with your fuckin' games!"

"Byron, listen."

"No more listening. The video goes to the cops! I got a few people who'll pay me hefty for this shit." Byron jumped out of the car and looked as if he was retreating back in the woods.

With that said, Nessa then looked over at Brandon realizing they were going to have to kidnap him. Brandon was already ahead of her though. Nessa motioned for Brandon to watch the car parked ahead. Two images emerged slightly. They looked like they were in a deep kiss and had possibly been smooching down in the seats shortly before being seen.

"It's just some trick bitch giving a nigga some head," Brandon stated as he hopped out of the car and stormed off toward Byron. Pulling his gun, he yelled Byron's name along with Nessa.

"Byron, wait!" Brandon shouted.

"Stop acting so childish," Nessa added. "We can work this out!"

Hearing his daughter's voice, Byron turned around.

Then the gun sounded.

Crack!!!!!

Crack!!!!!

Crack!!!!!

Nessa froze.

Three bright flashes exploded from Brandon's gun, each accompanied by hollow tipped bullets. All three bullets immediately tore into Byron's chest and sent him stumbling backwards. He fell to the ground.

Nessa's mouth dropped. She was totally speechless. She couldn't believe what she'd just seen.

Byron, still alive but just barely, turned over and began to pull himself along the ground in a last ditch effort to get away. As he pulled himself, his blood began to leave a trail underneath him and behind him along the surface of the pavement.

"Brandon, don't !" Nessa screamed.

Refusing to let Byron live, Brandon quickly strutted angrily towards him with his gun aimed.

"What the fuck are you doing?!" Nessa screamed while grabbing his arm.

Snatching away from her, Brandon made his way across the concrete to Byron. Taking aim at the back of his skull, Brandon squeezed the trigger. Dying instantly, Byron's brains were now scattered all over the ground.

"You son of a bitch!" Nessa screamed. She was hysterical. "I told you not to kill him. I fuckin' told your ass not to do it!"

Turning around and marching towards Nessa, Brandon yelled back, "It had to be done!"

"No, it didn't!"

Getting directly in Nessa's face, he screamed, "This is the fuckin' life you chose, Nessa. In order to reach the top in this game, you've got to murder the muthafuckas who are trying to hold you back!"

"But he was my father!"

"And Luke, Chetti, and Darien were my family. So, what the fuck about it? That blood is thicker than water shit don't fly in this game. It's dog eat dog, Nessa. Every beast for himself. *That's* how you survive!"

"Goddamn it, Brandon, this is *my* thing. I give the orders!"

Hearing those words made something shift inside Brandon. Developing a rabid expression across his face, he said, "Bitch, don't get it twisted. You may have power but I'm *powerful*. Big difference. I gave you everything. Me, bitch. And I can take it away if I feel the need to. Don't you ever fuckin' forget it."

65

Nessa stood seething. She didn't quite know how to respond to what he'd just said. She realized maybe it was best to not say anything.

Snatching Nessa's purse, Brandon took the fifty thousand from inside and tossed the purse on the ground. "This is to pay off the Mexicans."

Nessa still remained silent but pissed off as she watched Brandon turn and head to his car. As the engine came to life and he pulled away leaving her alone, she realized two things. One was that her relationship turned partnership with him was going to have to come to an end. And number two...

The car that had been parked across the street from the park was now gone.

Chapter-8

Outside the cabin a rented Chrysler 300 was parked near the front door. The sun beamed down over the cabin and surrounding trees. Inside, far beyond angry, Chetti paced back and forth across the floor holding a glass of Tequila in her right hand. Ice cubes clinked against the sides of the glass with each step she took. In her other hand she held a cigar; a Louixs, the best cigar money could buy. Smoke slithered from its lit end towards the ceiling.

Chetti, fresh out of jail, still looked just as beautiful as she did the very day she was arrested. Her hair was pulled back and nails freshly done. Dressed in a Chanel from head to toe, her facial expression showed her distaste for the flies buzzing around the dead bodies.

Sitting in a chair in the far corner of the room watching in silence was Mac, Chetti's most trusted bodyguard. Mac got his name because of his solid and rugged build, a build as indestructible as a Mac truck. He stood a towering 6'5". He weighed a little over three hundred pounds and was black as coal. His hands were huge and calloused. And he always kept a gun in close reach.

Mac, although a bodyguard, was a renaissance man of sorts for Chetti. He was a killer, kidnapper, hustler, and businessman. He'd been responsible for watching Chetti's money on the streets for years. And since Chetti had been gone, he'd been responsible for killing whoever she needed killed. He was also part of the reason she was now free. It was him who had hustled and grinded hard to get up the money for Chetti's release. The very moment Chetti's bond was made public, he posted the bail and was on the steps of the jail awaiting her and her attorney.

At the moment, besides Mac and Deena, no one knew Chetti was free. She wanted it to remain that way for a while. She had to plot and scheme for a moment. Aside from that, she was pissed the fuck off.

"Fucking incompetent sons of bitches!" Chetti yelled as she continued to pace the floor of the same cabin where Trinity and Cedrick had been held captive. She stepped over the decomposing bodies of the men she'd paid to handle her children as if their lives never mattered. "I gave those idiots two simple tasks. Just two: kill Trinity and watch over Cedrick. That was it. And what did those damn bozos do? Fuck it up!"

She took a pull from the cigar as she kept pacing. She was furious.

"Goddamn morons!" she hollered, smashing her foot onto the rotting face of one of her late goons. Blood oozed causing Mac to gag, yet Chetti never flinched.

Mac didn't say a word, just more gestures from the foul smell. He just sat in his chair keeping an eye on the window for anything or anyone suspicious. Although the cabin was miles away from civilization and no one knew Chetti was out yet, he wasn't taking any chances.

"If a bitch wants something done, she's got to do it her damn self!" Shaking her head, Chetti took a sip of the Tequila. Then she told Mac, "I can't have Trinity and Cedrick coming back to haunt me. You understand?"

He nodded. He had always been a man of only few words.

"I'm going to need you to find them and dispose of their asses just like you've been doing everyone else. I want their

asses wiped out. Until I can beat this damn case, I have to cut
ties with anyone who the damn Feds can manipulate into talking. I don't trust no damn body. I'll be damned if I let them take
me down."

"I got you, boss," Mac told her.

"I mean maids…drivers…friends…everybody!"

Mac nodded. With his heavy-set voice, he asked? "You
want a proper burial for Cheo and Mooch?"

"Hell fuckin' no!" she shouted, followed by the ugliest
grimace he'd seen her make in a while. "Those morons didn't do
as I instructed! Instead of killing Trinity they got themselves
killed…so why in the hell would I bury them! Feed them to the
wolves!"

Heading over to the window, she took another stress
filled pull of her cigar. Damn, how she'd missed the taste of its
smoke. She'd craved it many nights along with a drink while
she sat in that damn cage. Now staring through the cloudy veil
she'd exhaled in front of her, looking out into the woods, growing solemn as the hours passed. "Fucking children," she muttered with both anger and a twinge of sadness.

Mac watched her back.

"You spend your entire life sacrificing for them," she
continued. "You give them the world. You give them an excel-
lent life. You give them yourself. But what do they do in repay-
ment?" Her face twisted as she answered her own question.
"They turn around and cut deals with The Feds. They spill family secrets. They disobey."

Mac shook his head.

Silence.

A little over a minute passed.

Still looking out of the window, Chetti thought hard
about Darien. Memories of giving birth to him filled her head
along with lessons taught. She saw his smile. She heard his
voice. It all brought heavy sadness to her heart. What seemed
like a dark cloud fell over her.

"My baby," she whispered as she thought about what

Darien must've looked like after taking such a savage beating in jail and dying so mercilessly. She grimaced at the pain he must've endured after being shanked. Just to know he bled out like a pig left her heart broken. She could imagine the blood. She could imagine its smell. She'd heard he had died with his eyes open. The thought of him staring up at the ceiling of his cell unearthed her for a moment. She could feel a tear welling up. Refusing to show weakness, she took a sip of her drink, threw her shoulders back like a soldier and held her chin up as she accepted what she'd done. "Couldn't take a chance," she now said to herself. "I knew he was going to disappoint me just like the rest of them. I knew he'd break. I had to do what I had to do..."

"I had to have the guards kill him."

Those words were accompanied with silence. There was nothing more for Chetti to say about it. With conspiracy charges, drug trafficking charges, gun distribution charges, and racketeering charges just to name a few dangling over Chetti, she'd had Darien beaten and killed by the guards out of fear that he'd break. She knew he wasn't built for jail. She knew he'd never been too smart. Yes, he'd been loyal. And yes, he had been a momma's boy. But with so much time hanging over his head, Chetti believed it was only a matter of time before he'd spill his guts to the Feds. She couldn't have that. She couldn't take that chance.

"Every bitch for herself," Chetti said just before throwing back what was left in her glass. "Every bitch for herself."

Turning to Mac, she said, "Set up a meeting with Brandon. He knew the mansion was going to get hit and didn't say a thing. I want to know his fucking reasons. If they're not good, I'm going to kill him where he stands."

"No problem," Mac said.

"Also, it's high time I pay Luke's little ghetto bed winch Nessa a visit. Since he wants to turn on the family, I want his bitch to see what pain feels like up close and personal. I want to cut that tramp's throat from ear to ear nice and slow."

"Got it, boss."

"And find fuckin" Trinity and Cedrick!!!!!!!!" she blasted angrily. I want them brought to me," she ordered as her veins nearly popped from her neck.

Turning to the window once again, she smirked. Folding her arms across her breasts with the faces of Brandon, Nessa, and her remaining three children branded on her brain, she said...

"The bitch is back."

When the door of the plush office lobby opened and Cedrick walked in, the secretary was at her desk talking on the phone. Once her eyes set on Cedrick, her bottom jaw dropped to the floor. Her face drained of color. Not a word fell from her mouth. At that moment, an attorney, Richard Falou, walked into the lobby also with his head down in paperwork. Finally, raising his eyes and seeing Cedrick, he froze and dropped his paper-work to the floor. Just like the secretary, he looked like he'd seen a ghost. He was absolutely speechless.

The secretary was the first to speak. "Mr. Bishop?" she asked as if scared he *would* answer her.

"Cedrick?" Richard asked.

"Yes," Cedrick answered.

"But," Richard said. "But." He was so in shock he couldn't speak another word.

"You're supposed to be dead," the secretary said.

"Been getting that a lot lately," Cedrick told her with a smile.

"Is it really you?" Richard asked. The expression on his face was still marred with shock and disbelief.

"Yes."

Realizing he wasn't staring at a ghost or a mirage, Richard crossed the lobby floor and hugged Cedrick. "Everyone thought you were dead."

"I know. That's just the way my mother wanted it."

"What do you mean?"

"I need to talk to you in your office. It's important."

"Obviously," Richard said. Then after telling his secretary to hold all his calls, he accompanied Cedrick back to his office and closed the door.

Richard's office sat on the tenth floor of the downtown Washington building. It's window held a beautiful view of the downtown skyline. Its furniture was expensive and imported from France. One of its walls held a stoic but intimidating life size painting of the law firm's founding father, Mr. Reginald Falou dressed in a suit and sitting in a chair with almost a cold stare. It was obvious he had been a man of no nonsense or fear.

"Have a seat," Richard told Cedrick.

Cedrick sat in a high-backed chair in front of Richard's desk.

Heading around the desk to his chair, which was also high-backed and leather, Richard took off his suit jacket to expose a crispy white button down and black suspenders. Hanging his jacket over the back of his chair and sitting down, he said, "It's still strange to wrap my mind around the fact you're still alive. What's going on? Where have you been?"

"In a nutshell, my mother kidnapped me, faked my death and has been holding me hostage all this time while keeping me medicated."

"You can't be serious."

"Difficult to believe, I know, but it's definitely true."

"Why would she do something so horrible?"

"She wanted control of the family. And when she wants something, she's the type who won't let even her own blood stand in her way."

Cedrick went into detail about what he'd endured since the kidnapping. He also told Richard about Trinity's rape and molestation. As he did, Richard was aghast at what he was hearing. His face twisted in expressions of disgust with each word spoken. He'd heard a lot during his twenty-five years as an at-

72

torney, but what he was hearing now was by far the most troubling.

"She's an evil woman," Cedrick said ending the story. "Sick at that."

"Wow."

"Wow is an understatement."

"Obviously I'm assuming you're here to make sure charges can be brought against her to the fullest extent of the law. No problem. Let's get right on it."

"Actually, that's not why I'm here. It's not even on my mind."

Richard looked at him like he was crazy.

"Don't worry," Cedrick said. "I assure you she won't get away with what she did. I'll make absolute sure of that."

"Well, what can I help you with?"

"My inheritance."

"I see. The best way to get back at a person of wealth is to hit them in the pockets."

"Exactly, and I'm taking power over the family again."

"Well, as far as I know, all of the family's assets are under Federal freeze right now. But since you're the beneficiary and obviously it can't be proven that you had anything to do with the criminal activities, it shouldn't be difficult to get everything unfrozen."

"Good."

"We can get started on everything tomorrow morning."

"Thanks."

"How are you now? Where are you living?"

"With a friend. Both myself and Trinity are living there."

Reaching into his pocket he pulled out some cash and then handed it to Cedrick. "Take that. I know it's not much but it should help you for a little while. It's about nine hundred."

"Richard, I can't take your money."

"Cedrick, I can't hear of that. As much help as your father gave in helping to establish this firm, it's the least I can do."

Richard grabbed a pen and his checkbook, and made out

a check for two thousand dollars and handed it to Cedrick.

Cedrick sighed and accepted the check.

"Man, I appreciate it. I'll pay you back every penny."

"Nonsense. I won't hear of it. Now, let's discuss where we go from here," Richard said.

The two men began to discuss their plans to see to it that Cedrick would rise back to the top of the Bishop family. An hour later, Cedrick was exiting the building. Out on the busy street, the first thing he heard was a hotdog vendor yelling the prices of her hotdogs. He then couldn't help taking in the sounds of busy traffic. He couldn't believe he was back among all of it. Getting ready to go about his way, he noticed someone leaning against a car staring directly at him as if they knew him. Ignoring them, he attempted to head up the sidewalk.

"Cedrick Bishop!" someone called.

Cedrick turned to see the stranger who'd been leaning against the car heading towards him. Reaching Cedrick, the stranger said, "I'd heard a rumor but I didn't believe it was true. And if I hadn't expected it, I'd swear you were a ghost."

"How do you know my name?" Cedrick asked suspiciously. "Do I know you?"

"No, but I guarantee when I tell you who I am, and how I can assist you with your quest to get revenge on the people who had you locked in that room like a savage animal, you'll *want* to know me."

Cedrick was still skeptical but now intrigued.

"Who the hell are you?"

"Can we go somewhere and talk over a drink?" the stranger asked.

"Hell no, I don't even know you!"

"Trust me. It's in your best interest to know me."

Cedrick paused.

"Mr. Bishop, it'll be worth your while. Again...trust me."

"I don't trust anyone," he stated flatly.

"Well, does this change your mind?"

The stranger pulled the unthinkable from underneath the small pocket of a coat.

Seconds passed.

Then...Cedrick thought really hard.

"Alright," Cedrick finally said.

Filthy Rich-2 BY: KENDALL BANKS

Chapter - 9

The sound of the gun blasts still filled Nessa's ears. She could still see the flashes from its barrel. She could still see Byron pitifully pulling himself along the ground like a bleeding slug. It all nauseated Nessa. It nauseated her so badly, she'd thrown up several times over the past few days almost each time she thought about Byron's murder. His death was eating away at her constantly.

Nessa hadn't been able to sleep well. She hadn't been able to make it through her days with clear thoughts. Her conscience wouldn't allow her to. She felt totally responsible for Byron's death and it was tormenting her.

Of course Byron had been an asshole to Nessa. Of course he had been a deadbeat, con- artist, liar, and so much more. But despite all that, no matter how much Nessa hated the man he'd become, he was still her father. And she couldn't let go of that.

Heading to Chavez's for a re-up, Nessa stressfully rested the side of her head against her free hand as she drove with the other. The game wasn't quite starting out the way she'd hoped, she had to admit. The money was coming in but she could do without the damn drama.

"This is the life you chose!" Nessa could still hear Brandon screaming at her that night. "In order to reach the top in this game, you've got to murder the muthafuckas who are trying to hold you back!"

Those words rang loudly in Nessa's mind and ears. She knew they were true, but *damn*. She just couldn't get past Byron being the first one that had to be killed. It had her fuming at Brandon's actions. The son of a bitch had gone against her wishes. She knew that couldn't be tolerated but what exactly could she do about it? He was a Fed. If she killed him and got caught, she'd get the electric chair. If she simply stopped fucking with him, there was no end to what he could use his authority in his quest for revenge. The dilemma had her stressing hard.

Real hard.

"So, what are you going to do about the situation?" Piper now asked, sitting in the passenger seat. "This damn Brandon character is obviously a loose cannon."

"I don't know," Nessa answered, running her hand through her hair.

"What do you mean, you don't know?"

"I mean, I don't know." Nessa grew agitated.

"I know Byron was a piece of shit. And you'd better believe I won't miss him. Shit, the world is better off without him. But still, he wasn't supposed to be killed without your order to do it."

"You think I don't know that?"

"I don't know. It looks like you're letting this Brandon guy run over you. You're going to need to run a tighter ship. I mean damn, what type of popsicle stand are you running here?"

"Look, mom, all this was your damn idea in the first place."

"And I didn't see you complaining. You wanted the money just as bad as I did."

Growing more stressed, Nessa said, "Look, mom, I don't want to talk about this right now. I just brought you along so you could meet Chavez. That way, no matter what happens with the Brandon situation, you'll be locked in."

Piper sighed and shook her head. She was definitely displeased with Nessa right now but decided to let it go. Obviously, she had her own problems to be stressed about. She was still going to call Brandon later on though and check his ass.

Finally reaching the mansion, rolling through its parting gates, making their way up its winding drive way and parking at its steps, Nessa and Piper climbed out of the car and were escorted inside by several of Chavez's henchmen. As they walked, Nessa carried a duffel bag filled with five hundred thousand dollars that she'd picked up from Sidra's. It was the profit made by NaNa and his crew on the 17 bricks they'd bought and sold from Chavez .

It was time to re-up.

"Nessa," Chavez greeted her in his den. Arising from his chair behind the desk, he made his way around the desk, took Nessa's hand and kissed it like a gentleman. "An honor to do business with you again."

"Same here."

"And who's your friend?"

"This is actually my mother."

"Your mother?" Chavez had a strange expression spread across his face. He began twirling a massage ball through his fingers as he slipped into deep thought. "No Brandon?" he finally asked.

"He had to handle something."

"Nessa, I must insist that there be no more new faces. New faces make me nervous." His expression was serious, signaling although he was a gentleman, he wasn't to be tested.

"I understand."

Chavez stood hesitant. His eyes looked as though they were eyeing Piper up and down. Noticing their boss' reaction, the two goons at the door stepped forward exposing the guns underneath their suit jackets.

Nessa grew uneasy.

"Is there a damn problem?" Piper asked.

Not taking kindly to the disrespect Piper had just shown their boss, both men quickly pulled their guns and began to ap-

79

proach her.

Nessa's body tensed. She looked at her mother like she'd gone absolutely coo-coo for damn Cocoa Puffs.

Raising his hand to signal his goons to halt, Chavez eyed Piper a little more. The glare he was giving her was as if he knew her or had seen her somewhere before. A smile, although not quite a pleasant one, began to appear across his face. "What's your name?" he asked.

"Piper," she answered, obviously nervous but putting up a strong front.

Hearing the name, Chavez stroked his goatee for a brief moment while keeping his eye on Piper and seeming to be thinking about something. Nessa didn't like it. Something about it was creepy. Then signaling for his goons to head back to the door, he extended his hand to Piper and said, "You police?"

"Hell no!" Piper spat.

"Then it's an honor meeting you."

Piper accepted his hand.

Nessa noticed he didn't kiss it. Something about that struck her strangely.

Releasing Piper's hand, he said, "Please, ladies, have a seat."

Everyone sat at the desk.

"I'm assuming the bag contains my money?" Chavez asked.

"Yes," Nessa told him. "And a little more than before so I can get more product. Things are moving faster than I expected."

"Great, I can do each brick at a little over twenty-five a piece."

"That's ridiculous," Piper said.

Taken off guard, Chavez asked her, "Excuse me?"

Nessa immediately kicked her mother's ankle.

Ignoring Nessa, Piper said, "She paid a little under 17k for the last batch, and unloaded them quicker than your dick can get hard. Now here she is spending a half million with you once again, and you going up on the price! She's not spending chump change here, pretty boy! She deserves much cheaper prices."

Chavez eyed Piper with something unexplainable. Nessa couldn't tell if it was displeasure, contempt, anger or something else. It was difficult to read. All Nessa knew for sure was he didn't like Piper at all.

"Mom, can we step outside and talk?" Nessa asked.

"Nothing to talk about right now but this business," Piper said while continuing to look directly across the desk at Chavez. "And we don't have to step outside for that."

Silence.

Nessa could feel the stares of Chavez's henchmen burning a hole through the back of her head. Also, Chavez's demeanor and look ever since he first saw Piper; wasn't sitting well with Nessa. There was something about it.

A dark cloud seemed to have fallen over the den.

Acquiring a smile, Chavez asked Piper, "What price do you think is more suitable, uh, Piper is it?"

"Yes, and I think sixteen is more than fair."

"Sixteen grand?"

"Yup, that's what I said. So get ya feelings wrapped up and let's get this money."

Chavez leaned back in his chair, pulled out a cigar and then signaled for one of his men. A goon quickly walked over to him, lit his cigar and then headed back to the door. But not before giving both Nessa and Piper a look that easily revealed his thirst for his boss to give the order to have them killed. Seeing that look, Nessa just wanted to get the deal over with and go.

Moments passed.

"You are aware that my product is the most potent in the state?" Chavez asked Piper while exhaling smoke towards her as if purposely wanting to agitate her.

"Of course," she answered.

"So, it's well worth the asking price."

"Didn't say it wasn't."

"I just said my *daughter's* not paying it."

81

"Mom?" Nessa said.

Piper dismissed her with a wave of her hand while keeping an eye on Chavez. Then as if she hadn't disrespected him enough, she pulled out a pack of cigarettes, lit up without his permission, took a pull and then exhaled smoke across the desk towards him the exact same way he'd done her. Seeing that, Nessa's heart began to race.

Piper was getting ready to get them killed.

Moments passed.

Glares exchanged.

Finally, letting a smirk develop, Chavez said, "Twenty grand. Take it or leave it."

Quickly, Nessa said, "We'll take it."

Piper smirked also.

"Then we have a deal," Chavez said.

The three discussed more specifics. Moments later, the meeting was concluded and both Nessa and Piper were headed for the door. As they reached it, Chavez said from his desk, "Oh, and Piper?"

Piper turned to him.

"Make no mistake," he told her. "Although I'm a gentleman and I believe in treating women with the utmost respect, if you ever come into my home and light up another cigarette without my permission...I'll kill you."

The expression on his face was cold as ice.

Piper didn't respond.

Neither did Nessa.

Both knew it was best to keep their mouths shut at the moment. As they left, Chavez hopped on his cell. Nessa assumed it was to inform his boys of the location they were to drop the work off at. Whatever it was, she didn't care. She just wanted to get out of the mansion as soon as possible. Finally, in the car, she yelled, "Mom, what the fuck is wrong with you? Are you fuckin' crazy?!"

Shrugging it off, Piper said, "Don't worry about it. I know his type. You've got to play hardball with him."

"I know his type, too. He's the type to blow your damn head off if you cross him."

"So, you think he would've actually killed you, Nessa? Do you think he would've compromised a five hundred thousand dollar deal?"

"He could've just killed us and took the money."

"He's a businessman, Nessa. Trust me; he wants the long term money. I swear you've got a lot to learn about this shit. No wonder this Brandon character is taking advantage of you."

"He's not taking advantage of me," she fired back. "I play dumb for all those idiots who underestimate me. When the time comes, I'll shock everybody."

"Ummm hmmm," Piper mocked. "Tell that shit to somebody who's listening."

Shaking her head and not wanting to hear anymore, Nessa pulled away from the mansion's steps and headed towards the Southeast part of D.C. Reaching it about thirty minutes later, the neighborhood seemed even shadier than the last drop off spot. Pulling to a curb, Nessa placed her gun on her lap and waited. Ten minutes later an SUV different from the last one appeared across the street. Just like last time, two young boys got out with book bags, jogged across the street and gave the bags to Nessa. Moments later, they were back in the SUV and gone. Satisfied, Nessa began to pull away from the curb.

Suddenly, three Dodge Challengers pulled up out of nowhere and boxed her in. Their doors opened immediately. Several Mexicans with Choppers jumped out. Each had their guns pointed directly at Nessa and Piper.

"Put your fuckin' hands up, bitches!" a goon demanded.

Both Nessa and Piper did as they were told. As they did, Nessa recognized one of the men. It was Londo, the Mexican Brandon had made the deal with. She now watched him approach her car with his gun aimed. She was terrified and pissed all at the same time. *That fuckin' snake ass Brandon*, she said to herself.

"This some bullshit!" Piper shouted.

Snatching the door open, Londo asked, "Where's the dope, holmes?"

"What shit?"

"Mira, stop fucking playing, holmes."

Placing the gun to her forehead, he yelled, "You know what I'm talking about, punta. Play cute again and I'll paint the inside of this car with your blood. One to your cabesa, bitch. Now where's the shit!"

Piper eyed Nessa. She wanted her to say nothing at all.

"In the back seat," Nessa fired.

"Damn it! Nessa," Piper screamed.

As soon as she said that, the back door was snatched open and the bags were removed.

"Fuck! Fuck! Fuck!" Nessa yelled. "Why are you doing this? I paid you what you asked."

Nessa figured that Brandon had fucked her over…she just needed confirmation.

Chuckling, the Mexican said, "You paid me, huh?"

"Yes."

"Seems you and your boy Brandon have your wires crossed, holmes. He didn't pay me shit. That's why I'm hittin' your ass up, punta."

Nessa shook her head rapidly then landed it harshly against the steering wheel.

Heading back to his Challenger, the Mexican yelled to Nessa, "When you see Brandon again, tell him I want that connect. If I don't get it, your dope won't be the only thing I take!"

With that said, the Challengers all sped off leaving Nessa robbed and disgusted. Piper said nothing. Nessa could not believe her mother was acting so passive after she just told her how soft she was.

Exiting FBI Headquarters, Brandon headed across the parking lot towards his car. As he made his way across the lot, his phone was pinned to his ear.

"You back stabbing punk!" Nessa's voice screamed angrily from the other end of the phone. "Why didn't you pay them?"

"Because your ass needed to learn a lesson," Brandon told her. "You got shit twisted the other night."

"What the fuck are you talking about?"

"We're a team. But you've been trying to treat me like you're running shit," he said, pressing the phone closer to his ear. He kept turning around to watch his back.

"Brandon, you're fuckin' trippin'!"

"You won't tell me where the money is stashed. You won't tell me how much money is being made. You're disappointing me, Nessa."

"You unappreciative muthafucka!"

"Oh, it's *me* who's unappreciative? Wasn't it me who helped you make this happen? Wasn't it me?"

Nessa, didn't answer.

"And don't get it twisted," he continued. "If it wasn't for me, you'd be dead right now. Every fucking goon and cut throat would be taking a chunk out of your ass. Who do you think is responsible for allowing you to move worry free? Me, that's who."

"Brandon! Listen to me!"

"No, Nessa. You listen and you listen good. From here on out, I want in on everything. I want to *know* everything, including where the money gets stashed. If I don't start getting some satisfaction, them crazy ass Cholos will be the *least* of your fuckin' worries."

"Brandon!" she shouted again.

No response.

The call ended.

Reaching his car and shoving the phone in his pocket, Brandon pulled out his keys. Placing one in the door, he didn't notice the Chrysler 300 approaching him. Just as he turned the lock on his door, the car stopped behind him. The door opened.

Mac appeared and quickly made his way towards Brandon. Throwing Brandon in a headlock and dragging him backwards like a ragdoll, he pulled him towards the trunk of the 300.

"What the hell is going on?" Brandon demanded, barely able to breathe while reaching in his jacket for his gun.

Mac punched Brandon in the belly with a blow so hard it knocked the air out of him. He then grabbed Brandon's gun, opened the trunk and tossed him inside. Mac carefully watched his back for any unsuspecting eyes. Seconds later, Mac hopped back into the driver's seat and pulled off.

Brandon was terrified as he pounded on the inside of the trunk screaming for help. He had no idea what was going on or why he'd been kidnapped. He was totally surprised also that whatever the reasons, the henchman had the nerve to do it to a Fed in the parking lot of the damn headquarters.

What seemed like forever passed.

Brandon lay in total darkness. He felt claustrophobic. He felt like he was going to run out of air at any moment and suffocate. And even if he didn't, he had a strange feeling once the trunk opened, he'd be killed. His life began to pass in front of his eyes.

More moments passed.

Finally, the car came to a stop.

Brandon listened closely as the car shut off. His eyes roamed the darkness as he listened to the car's driver door open and shut. He then heard footsteps make their way from the driver's door to the trunk. His heart began pounding at what was about to happen. Over the pounding of his heart, he then heard the keys enter the trunk's lock and turn.

Then, the trunk opened.

Bombarded by sunlight, he squinted his eyes. But only for a brief second. The face of the person standing beside his kidnapper made him widen them in surprise and fear.

"You've got explaining to do, Brandon," Chetti said, standing beside Mac.

"Chetti, how did you get out?" Brandon asked.

"All that's not important. What *is* important is that you didn't tell me about the raid beforehand."

Talking fast, he said, "Chetti, I swear to God I didn't know they were going to hit."

"That's not what I heard."

"I swear, I didn't."

Mac pulled out a gun.

"Chetti, please," Brandon begged. "You've got to believe me."

"I don't *got* to do a damn thing but stay pretty and die."

"Chetti, hear me out."

"You knew about the investigation and you knew about the raid. That's the word I got. And my sources have never been wrong."

Mac cocked the gun.

"Okay, I knew about the investigation," Brandon admitted quickly. "But I swear I didn't know about the raid. I didn't know until the last second. They didn't want to take a chance on there being a rat so they didn't let most of us know exactly where we were heading until we were pretty much there. By then, it was too late to warn you. I swear, Chetti. I swear to God!"

Chetti shook her head. "You disappointed me, Brandon."

"I was going to get you out of jail. I really was. In fact, I've been hustling hard with Nessa to get your bail money."

"Nessa?"

"Yes."

"Luke's Nessa?"

"Yes." He reached into his suit jacket's inner pocket.

Mac quickly placed the gun to his forehead. "What the fuck you reaching for?"

Holding his hands up defensively and in fear, Brandon said, "Not a gun. Just want to show Chetti I'm not lying."

"What you got to show me?" Chetti asked.

"Slow, nigga," Mac said. "Do it slow."

"No problem," Brandon said. He then reached into his

87

pocket and pulled out the fifty thousand he'd taken from Nessa.

"What's this?" Chetti asked.

"Just a little something but there's more where it came from."

Chetti took the money.

"After I found out that Luke was turning on you, I talked Nessa into turning on him. He had money stashed. I talked her into stealing it. She's flipping it right now as we speak. As soon as she got it flipped, I was going to kill her ass and get you out of jail."

Chetti was listening carefully.

"I swear, Chetti," he continued. "I would never cross you. You're like a mother to me."

Still looking at the money in her hand, Chetti asked, "How's your relationship with Nessa?"

"I'm playing that bitch like a puppet."

Coming up with an idea, Chetti told him, "Well, keep it that way. I need that bitch to get as much money out here as possible."

Chetti realized she could rise back to the top of the game with no hard work at all. All she had to do was sit back and collect. With Nessa not knowing that Brandon was on Chetti's side, she would be playing on Chetti's team without even knowing it. She'd be taking all the chances. And then when Chetti no longer needed her, she could turn the lights out on that bitch. And Nessa would never see it coming.

Chetti smiled.

"Chetti, I never betrayed you. I swear I didn't," Brandon continued.

"Fuck all that," she interrupted. "You just make sure from here on out, Nessa makes every move possible to rise to the top of the game. When I come to regain my throne, I want it nice and shiny."

With that said, Chetti turned and walked off. Future riches filled her thoughts. The only other thing she thought about was her meeting with Chavez. From what he'd told her earlier when he called, he had something very important to tell her, something he assured her she would want to hear.

He now had her overly curious.

Filthy Rich-2 BY: KENDALL BANKS

Chapter - 10

The state of the art exercise room was scarcely populated with old white men in sweat suits and sneakers. Their crimes, although felonious, were mainly white collar. Most of them were rich men who'd bilked people out of their life's savings, retirements, and 401Ks. There was no remorse in them. If anything, the only thing they were sorry for was that they'd gotten caught.

As a few of the men spoke to each other while on exercise bikes and treadmills, they spoke about their schemes and their regrets that they'd gotten too greedy at points where they should've pulled out sooner. If they'd pulled out, they wouldn't be sitting in prison for decades being punished for taking innocent, elderly people for every penny they had ever worked for, let alone their houses and their grandchildren's college tuitions.

Among the men, Luke couldn't help ear hustling as he jogged on a treadmill while a flat screen television played on a front wall several yards in front of him. As he listened to the men, he couldn't believe their arrogance. He couldn't believe their lack of remorse. If there was one thing Luke couldn't stand, it was folks who preyed on people who couldn't quite defend themselves. That shit always got underneath his skin.

Luke wasn't an angel of course. He was the furthest thing from it. But he had morals. He had a fear of karma. It was because of those things that he only believed in inflicting revenge on those who were involved in the same game he played, not innocent civilians. It was Chetti and Darien who believed even a person's children were up for grabs if the family was crossed. It was them who'd give the order to murder a mother on a Sunday morning directly in front of church if her son stole from them. Luke could never give that type of order.

An officer walked into the exercise room and headed towards Luke. Reaching him, he said, "Mr. Bishop, you've got a visitor."

"Alright," Luke told him. "Let me get a quick shower first."

The officer nodded.

Luke grabbed a towel, wiped sweat from his forehead and headed off to the shower. Moments later, in a new sweat suit, he was headed across the yard with the officer by his side. Reaching the visiting area, he assumed it was either the Feds or an attorney who was there to see him. It couldn't have been Pamela because all her visits with him took place at the trailers.

The visiting room was filled with dozens of steel tables and benches. Several vending machines lined its walls. Televisions overhung from all for corners of the room. Magazine stands also lined the walls.

"Sit anywhere," the officer told Luke.

Luke sat at a table in the center of the room. A distance away through a window, he could see the trees that surrounded the compound as the sun shined over them. For a moment, he yearned for the life he had beyond those trees.

A door opened.

Luke turned to see who was entering the room. When he saw who it was, he thought his eyes were deceiving him for a moment. He thought it was a mirage. He just couldn't believe it. But as the person began to head towards him, he knew for sure it wasn't a mirage or a figment of his imagination. It really was Cedrick.

Practically leaping from his chair, Luke grabbed his

brother and hugged him tightly. "Man, I thought you were dead," he told him. "I thought she'd killed you."

Cedrick didn't hug his brother back. Instead, he kept his arms at his sides. He had no interest in returning his brother's affections.

Finally, realizing his brother wasn't hugging him back, reality struck Luke like lightning. He realized he wasn't worthy of his brother's hugs. He wasn't even worthy of his brother's visit. Realizing all that, he slowly let his brother go, stepped back and looked at him. In Cedrick's eyes he saw darkness, displeasure, and more. Sighing and wishing things could be different, Luke said, "My whereabouts are secret. No one is supposed to know I'm here. How'd you know?"

"Let's just say someone in the FBI granted me a favor," Cedrick told him without changing the expression on his face.

"Brandon?"

Cedrick didn't answer. He just stared at his brother. Silence.

After several moments, Luke stuffed his hands into the pockets of his sweat pants, turned and headed to the window. Looking outside, he said, "I know it may not mean much but I came looking for you the day the mansion was raided."

"To cover your own ass?"

"No, to set you free."

"Too little too late."

Luke couldn't say anything else.

"Who's idea was it to kidnap me?" Cedrick asked.

"Mother's."

"But you and Darien went along with it."

"What other choice did we have?"

"The *right* fucking choice!" Cedrick yelled angrily. "I was your damn brother for God's sake!"

With his back still to his brother, Luke said, "And if we had made the *right* choice as you say, what do you think she would've done to *us*?"

Shaking his head, Cedrick said, "So, rather than die

93

yourself for doing the right thing, the two of you decided to let me sit in that room and die day after, day after, day for trying to do the right thing for the family, huh?"

The truth pained Luke. He closed his eyes and grimaced.

"Do you know what she put me through in that room, Luke? Do you know the things she did to me? Do you know the torture?"

Luke continued to keep his eyes closed. The darkness behind his eyelids somehow made the moment easier to deal with. His heart and conscience was still killing him though.

"Yeah," Cedrick continued. "I think you know. In fact, I'm *sure* you know seeing as how you're the father of our own baby sister's child."

Luke grimaced again in shame. The truth cut like a knife. It cut all the way through to his soul and further.

"Yeah, you know what that sick bitch did to me. It was hell, a hell that you played a part in locking me in."

Luke couldn't speak. He couldn't turn to face his brother knowing he'd failed him terribly. He'd betrayed him and didn't look back. Up until the moment just before the raid, all he had thought about was himself. Now he was truly ashamed of himself for being so selfish.

"Don't worry about it though," Cedrick said. "I didn't come here to argue and point fingers. I just came to let you know to enjoy the ride ahead of you."

Luke opened his eyes and turned.

"Seeing you sit in here isn't satisfaction enough for me, Luke, especially now that I've discovered you've cut a deal that will most likely allow you back on the streets again. No, I'm not satisfied."

Both brothers eyed each other.

"What's going to satisfy me is seeing the look on your damn face, Luke, when you have no idea what is coming finally collides with you. There's a huge shit storm coming. When it does, there will be no deals. There will be no way to hide or run. When it happens, what you've lost up until this moment will in

94

absolutely no way compare to what you will lose *then*."

Luke listened in silence. His ears had never been more focused on someone's words than they were at that moment.

"*That's* when I'll be satisfied, Luke. And mark my words, little brother. It's coming."

With those words spoken, Cedrick stood up.

"Cedrick, we've got to stick together, bro. Did you hear what happened to Darien last week?"

"No, and don't care," Cedrick muttered as he turned and left the room leaving Luke with silence to bare, inner demons to battle and a curiosity of what his brother meant by "You have no idea what is coming until it finally collides with you."

Luke dropped his head.

The door opened.

Footsteps quickly made their way across the floor to Luke.

"Mr. Bishop?"

"Yeah,"

"Look, I shouldn't be telling you this but…"

Officer Flippen stopped before speaking further.

Looking at the officer, Luke asked, "What is it?"

With a nervous expression on his face mixed with worry, the officer looked at the door and then back at Luke. Stepping closer to Luke, Flippen whispered, "There's been a rumor going around among the officers. It's bad for you."

"What?"

"Well…"

The door opened.

The burly Sargent with a massive amount of pimples spread across his cheeks appeared at the door. "Officer Flippen," he said.

"Yes."

"I'll take Mr. Bishop back to his cell."

"But, I thought I was taking him back."

"You're relieved, Sir."

The officer paused for a moment. He then looked at Luke

with a weird countenance and with eyes that silently said, 'You'd better watch your back.' He then walked off. Officer Flippen would prove to be an ally for Luke but he had no idea why.

As Luke headed across the yard and back to his cell with the Sargent beside him, he couldn't get the officer's words and the expression out of his head. It was obvious something was up. Luke knew it definitively. Why else would a Sargent go out of his way to walk him back to his cell?

Nessa stormed into Sidra's living room pissed off. "Fuck," she screamed. "That damn snake!"

Piper walked into the house behind her.

"What's goin' on?" Sidra asked.

"That bastard, Brandon!"

"What about him? What'd he do?"

"He didn't pay the damn Mexicans!"

Sidra shook her head.

"Since he didn't pay 'em, they just caught me in traffic and got me for all the product I just got from Chavez!"

"Damn, Nessa, that was a lot of money! All gone down the drain." Sidra plopped down on the couch, leaned back into its cushions and began massaging her temples.

"Well, shit, Nessa, you can't let that muthafucka get away with this shit."

"Damn right she can't," Piper co-signed.

"Plus, you know NaNa is going to want his cut regardless."

Silence filled the room.

Growing annoyed with everything around her, Nessa stood and began to pace. "Shit, that's a heavy fuckin' loss," she stated under her breath. Things were just starting to get rolling for her.

Sidra reached underneath a cushion of the couch and pulled out a gun. Since she started holding money for Nessa, she started making sure to keep pistols stashed. Never knew when a muthafucka might decide to try and kick her door in. Now waiving the gun, she yelled, "I say we get that sneaky son of a bitch, cut his balls off, put a hole in his head and dump his ass in the water!"

"Calm down, Sidra," Nessa told her while still pacing.

"She's right, Nessa," Piper agreed. "You can't let his ass get away with this shit."

"Mom, don't start."

"I told you that was what your problem was. You're too damn passive, too soft."

"Mom!"

"Don't mom, me. To make it out here, you've got to be a vicious bitch."

"Hell fuckin' yeah," Sidra agreed. "If the streets find out you let the Mexicans cross you, everyone's goin' to come after you."

"You'll be a target." Piper began coughing. Amidst the coughing, she said, "You've got to get these muthafuckas." Her coughing then grew heavier and raspy, causing her to bend over.

"You okay?" Sidra asked.

Piper continued coughing. Sitting on the couch, she reached into her pocket and pulled out a handkerchief. Placing it to her mouth, she coughed into it. Pulling it away from her mouth slightly and at an angle that only she could see, she looked at it and saw blood. Quickly, she wiped her mouth and stuffed it back into her pocket.

Looking at her mother, Nessa asked, "Are you okay?"

"Yeah, I just need a cigarette."

"A cigarette?" Sidra asked in disbelief. "You just had such a deep cough, it sounded like someone was outside tearing up the streets."

"Just give me a cigarette, bitch."

"No, I'm not contributing to your death," Nessa fired.

97

"Goddamn it!" Piper screamed. "Just give me a fuckin' cigarette. Is that too much to ask?"

Both Nessa and Sidra looked at each other for a moment. Sidra then went into her purse, got out a pack of smokes and handed them to Piper. Accepting them, Piper removed one from the pack and lit up. Then going back to the point she was stressing a moment ago, she said, "You've got to tighten your shit, Nessa. We've come too fuckin' far to let it go down the drain."

"What, you think I don't know that?"

"I can't tell."

"Nessa, we've got to move on these muthafuckas," Sidra chimed in.

"Look," Nessa told them. "I already know that. Trust me; Brandon isn't going to get away with what he did. But getting his ass has to be done right. We can't just blow his head off. He's a Fed. They give bitches the chair for shit like that. We're going to have to deal with his ass in a special way."

"How?" Sidra asked.

"I'll figure it out."

"What about them wetbacks?"

"They'll definitely be dealt with. Them muthafuckas got me for all my shit. There's no way I'm going to let them get away with it."

Memories appeared in Nessa's head, memories of her father before the drugs and the streets took him under. She could remember overhearing him with his goons plotting and planning like a general on niggas who crossed him. Before he fell off, he never rushed into anything. He always planned first.

"My father might be an asshole," Nessa said, speaking as if he was still alive. "But if there's anything I learned from him, it's to never leave shit to chance. Always plan it out."

Piper rolled her eyes as she took another puff from her cigarette.

That moment caused Nessa to realize at some point she'd have to tell Piper about her father's murder and murderer. For now she couldn't. Nessa finally realized she had been moving all wrong. She had been naïve in certain areas. She had been short on calculating things. All that had stopped now. It was time she started operating smartly.

"Well, what now?" Sidra asked.

"Gotta get some more work from Chavez."

"Alright, I'll go get the remaining money from upstairs. It's about two hundred fifty grand. It's the last of it. "

"Nope."

"Why?"

"Not going to need it."

"How do you figure?"

"Another thing the old bastard taught me was to use what I *have* in order to get what I *want*."

Sidra looked at her friend skeptically.

"That money stays stashed. For a man like Chavez, I've got something just as valuable as money."

Realizing what her daughter was implying, a smile appeared on Piper's face behind a veil of cigarette smoke. After a moment, the realization of what her friend meant finally registered on Sidra's face also...

Pussy.

A man's quickest downfall.

"Look-a-here, I agree that pussy is power, but a man like Chavez wants money too," Sidra added.

Nessa pulled her phone from her pocket to call Chavez and set up another meeting.

Still smiling, Piper told her, "But at least you're using your damn head. Pussy is a powerful thing, baby!" she said, rubbing her hand in between her legs.

As soon as Chavez answered, Nessa put on her most innocent sounding voice. She even sounded like she was whimpering.

Hearing the trouble in Nessa's voice, Chavez asked, "You fucked up, didn't you?"

With Piper and Sidra watching her, still sounding like she was crying, Nessa said, "Chavez, I'm...I'm... I'm in trouble. The worst thing just happened to me. I didn't know who else to call but you."

"What's wrong? And don't talk crazy on my line."

"No one can be trusted," she sniveled.

"What happened?"

"I was robbed."

"By who?"

Nessa went into an act of heavy whimpering.

"Nessa?"

"Chavez, I owe people. Now without the barbies, I don't know what to do."

Chavez loved that fact that Nessa knew not to use certain words over the phone.

"Come see me," he said quickly, with disappointment lingering in his tone.

"I don't have any money."

"Just come see me."

"When?"

"Tomorrow evening."

Music to Nessa's ears.

After several moments, the two ended their conversation.

"Well?" Sidra asked.

Dropping the act and sounding normal again, Nessa smiled and said, "He wants me to meet him tomorrow evening."

"Bitch please. You think it's that easy?" Piper asked with a roll of the neck and eyes.

"Yep, and I'm gonna suck and fuck every last one of those bricks I lost right out of his ass," Nessa said.

"I hope you're right," Sidra added. "Something just doesn't seem right." Her head kept nodding as her body language became weirder.

Piper noticed the strange look on Sidra's face but decided not to say anything. She knew she'd have to keep an extra eye on Nessa's so called girl.

Chapter-11

Obviously Trinity had been through a lot lately. She'd lost her son brutally, a death and loss which she knew she would never get over. She'd been raped and almost killed, an act set up by her very own damn mother. She'd discovered her brother, whom she thought was dead, was still alive. And now, she'd just finished replacing the bandages from her recent hospital visit. Thank God her AIDS test was negative; along with the testing for other venereal diseases.

Trinity stood in the mirror staring at her reflection. Bruises, scratches and cuts filled all images. As she watched in sadness, she didn't know what to feel most: anger, betrayal, sadness, heartbreak, bitterness. There was so much going on inside her, so much pulling her in various directions.

From childhood, Trinity had learned to harden herself. Because of the abuse, she'd learned to close herself off. She'd learned to barbwire her heart. She'd learned to conceal her emotions. That was the only way she could be strong enough to deal with everything she'd been forced to face. That was the only way she got through. It had become her defense mechanism and in time, a total part of her, a part she relied on day after day.

Hardening herself hadn't always been Trinity's defense mechanism. It hadn't always been her means to cope. In the beginning, she cut herself with razors constantly, in-between the molestation and abuse. She even tried to kill herself by swallowing a half a bottle of pills.

Staring into the mirror, so many memories now bombarded Trinity; each of them painful. She saw molestation. She saw death. She saw Chetti beating her as a child with extension cords, broom handles, and poles while spitting on her and calling her worthless. She saw pure hell, a world no human being, especially an innocent child, should ever have to see.

The outside world never saw Trinity's scars. They never saw her bruises. Chetti wouldn't allow them to. She kept Trinity sheltered with home schooling, nannies, and personal doctors. She refused to take a chance on letting the world discover the torment she was inflicting on her daughter.

Trinity's knees now went weak and began to buckle. Everything on her mind and heart right now was just too much to bear. Before long, she collapsed to the floor of the bathroom and began crying harder than she could ever remember. The tears were flowing like a river. Angrily she pounded her fist against the wall beside her. She gritted her teeth. She growled like an animal. Veins protruded from her neck.

Trinity could see her mother's face in her mind. She could hear her devil filled laugh. She could see the men raping her in the cabin. She could feel the pain of them thrusting inside her over and over again. The memory made her pull her knees to her chest, rest the back of her skull against the wall behind her and thud it several times on purpose until she could feel a headache approaching. So bitter and so angry, she placed her face in her hands and whimpered like a newborn baby. It was all she could do right now to make it through the moment of having so much fury and rage flowing through her veins.

A knock came at the door.

"Trinity?" Cedrick called.

Trinity didn't answer. She kept her face in her hands. Her emotions had a grip on her that she couldn't break free from at the moment. She was completely lost in them.

Another knock.

"Trinity?"

Finally, Trinity raised her face from her hands. Her vision was heavily blurry. "Yeah?" she asked.

"You okay?"

She wiped the tears away. "Yeah."

"You sure?"

Yes, I'm good."

She stood while continuing to wipe the tears from her face. Tossing the pills she'd been hiding in her purse, and then quickly washing her face, she gave her reflection a look in the mirror once again. She could only sigh. Seconds later, she opened the door.

Seeing his sister, Cedrick could see the tracks of her tears despite the fact that she'd washed them away. He could see the redness of her eyes. He could see her hurt and pain.

The brother and sister duo stared at each other.

"If you need to talk, you know I'm here, right?" he asked.

She nodded.

"I'm not going anywhere ever again."

Those words comforted her.

"You sure you're okay?" he asked again.

"Now I am."

They hugged.

Immediately those weird feelings filled Trinity again. For some reason she thought of Cedrick as being her husband; the man who would protect her and caress her when needed. She looked deeply in his eyes and smiled the moment he placed a kiss on her forehead.

"You ready to go?" he asked releasing her.

"Yeah."

Moments later, the two were walking outside Amelia's door, and hopping into the rental car headed downtown.

"So, where are we going anyway?" she asked.

"Got somebody I need you to talk to."

"Who?"

"You'll see."

Accepting that he wasn't going to tell her more, Trinity leaned back in her seat and stared out of the window at the passing outside world. As she watched people go on about their lives, she wondered if any of them had a life as bad as hers. The thoughts were so stressful that she had to smoke a cigarette to ease her mind.

Moments passed.

The car was silent.

Eventually the rental made its way into downtown Washington. As it did, traffic busily rushed up and down the maze like streets. Men and women conversed with each other or into their cell phones as they made their way along the sidewalks. Eventually the rental pulled into the parking lot of FBI Headquarters.

Looking around, Trinity asked, "What are we doing here?"

As Cedrick parked the car, Trinity stared at him perplexed. Seeing her uncertainty, he said, "Don't worry. Everything's good."

Believing him, she put out her cigarette.

The two stepped out of the car and headed across the lot. Moments later, after having their new IDs checked, and having to pass through a metal detector, they were on an elevator. Stepping off, and walking by neatly dressed agents with holstered guns on their hips, and entering a lobby, Cedrick told Trinity to have a seat. As she did, he approached a secretary and told her who he was there to see. She nodded and got on the phone. After several seconds, she hung up and said, "They're expecting you. I'll escort you back there."

Cedrick and Trinity followed the secretary through a hall behind her desk. Seconds later, they were entering a conference room. A man and a woman, both agents, were awaiting them at the far end of a conference table.

The secretary left.

"Cedrick, glad you could make it," the female agent said. She was the agent who'd met Cedrick outside his attorney's office, the agent who'd been keeping a close eye on the Bishops for several months. More importantly, she was the agent who'd been keeping an eye on Luke. She was Pamela, fictitiously, Pamela Benson.

Her real name was Agent Linda Pierce.

"And this is Trinity, of course?" she asked.

Trinity looked at her and then at Cedrick. She had no idea what was going on.

"You gave us quite a scare the day of the raid, Trinity," Pamela's partner, Agent Logan, a young, white outspoken agent said, "We thought you were dead."

Trinity didn't say anything.

"Please have a seat," he said, running his hand through his stringy hair.

Both Cedrick and Trinity sat down at the end of the table.

"What's this about?" Trinity asked Cedrick.

"They want to help us," he told her.

"We know you want revenge," Agent Pierce stated.

Trinity stared down the table at her.

"We had a long talk with your brother, Cedrick. We know about the abuse and molestation. We know about what happened to you at that cabin. We know your mother sent you off to die."

Trinity didn't speak.

"We even know about your son, Gavin. That particular info we'd known about before we talked to Cedrick."

Tears welled up in Trinity's eyes.

"Sorry for your loss," Agent Pierce uttered. She paused a moment before continuing. "We've also completed a blood test on Gavin in regards to our investigation of your family. His blood matched with Luke's so we do have confirmation."

"So, wait...how long have you been investigating my family? And what do you want?" Trinity asked tensely.

"We've had your family under investigation for nearly a

105

year now," Logan said. "We picked up a whole lot on them: conspiracy, murder, trafficking, kidnapping; the works."

"So, what does that have to do with me?" she asked,
switching her temperament to a major attitude. She hated cops.

"Just hear them out, Trinity," Cedrick chimed in.

She sighed but listened.

"After the bust, your mother started killing off anyone
who could talk," Pierce continued. "That complicated our case.
Up until that point, our case against your family was based on
witnesses. But with those witnesses now dead, we have no one.
We can't even get to her supplier right now. Even the fact that
your brother Luke has now agreed to testify against your mother
isn't quite carrying importance. Without witnesses, it's his word
against hers. Also, the last thing we want to do is let Luke walk.
We want him just as bad as we want Chetti."

"You still haven't told me what this has to do with me."

"We need you to testify about the abuse and molestation.
We need you to testify about what was done to you at that cabin,
and that Chetti ordered it."

She shook her head. "I'd rather deal with them on my
own. Jail is too good for them."

"We understand but…"

"You don't understand. You'll never be able to understand. It happened to *me,* not *you!*"

"You're right, Trinity. I can't fully understand your pain.
But I *can* understand your thirst for revenge. Let us get it for
you. Let us take them down. Help us, Trinity."

Trinity grew silent. She didn't quite know what to do or
say. She wanted revenge. She wanted Chetti and Luke to pay for
her pain. But her dilemma was that she was torn between wanting their blood and wanting them to die in prison.

"We've even got your cousin, Brandon, committing ille-
gal activities on camera. We're hoping to eventually use that
against him to turn on your mother."

"He'll never do it," Trinity said with contempt.

"That's what you think," Agent Pierce said with a grin.

"How about the fact that we had two agents following him, and they saw him kill a man? You think him going to jail for murder will make him give us the info we want?"

Trinity shrugged her shoulders.

"Oh, he will go to jail, for life. We're just building our investigation. We just move cautiously when it involves arresting one of our own."

"Got something we need you to see, also," Logan interrupted.

"What?"

He grabbed a remote and clicked a button. A nearby television came to life. Seconds later, on its screen appeared Charles Bishop, Cedrick and Trinity's father. He was tied to a chair, his body battered and bloody. Loud cursing and yelling could be heard. Then Nessa's face appeared.

"What the..." Trinity muttered, leaning forward with her eyes glued to the screen.

The video continued to play.

No one spoke.

All eyes were on the screen.

Then, Mr. Bishop's throat was slit.

Trinity stood from her chair and turned. She began breathing hard and fast. Anger over took over her. "That lying, sneaky *bitch*!" she screamed, speaking of Nessa.

Everyone watched her carefully.

Trinity couldn't believe Nessa had the nerve to sit in her face and talk to her like the two were sisters when she knew all along she'd murdered her father. It wasn't that Trinity was upset because she too wanted to murder her father. It was principal. She couldn't believe Nessa lied to her.

"Where'd you get that video?" she turned to them and asked, seeing absolute red.

"That's not important," Pierce told her. "What's important is we have it. We're taking her down right along with your mother, Chetti, Luke and your cousin Brandon. We're devoted to this case. But we want *everyone*, not just a few."

Trinity didn't say anything. She was so overcome with fury. This was so much to dissect right now, especially Nessa. Yes, Trinity's father had molested her. But strangely, Trinity still loved him. She had always felt that Chetti manipulated him into molesting her. She still saw herself as daddy's little girl.

The room suddenly felt small. Trinity began to feel like she couldn't breathe. Suddenly, she snatched the door open and stormed out into the hall. Moments later, she was on the elevator. Before she knew it, she was out in the parking lot underneath the sun feeling overwhelmed. Everything around her seemed to spin. She felt like she was on a carousel.

"Trinity!" Cedrick called, jogging up behind her.

Turning to him, Trinity screamed, "She killed him, Cedrick. That bitch killed him!"

"I know sis, Agent Pierce told me yesterday. I hadn't seen the footage, but she warned me."

"Don't you care!" she shouted.

"I do. I do care. But I have so much running through my brain right now, I can't get side-tracked. Cedrick tried to take his sister in his arms but she refused him. Pulling away, she said, "I can't believe this shit!" We have to do something!"

"We will, Trinity. But for now, I have to focus on gaining control of this family and our fortune. I have no intentions on going to jail and losing it all. And I'll never lose you again. You hear me?"

Trinity was in tears. "I have to think, Cedrick. I just need time to think," she said, backing away from her brother like he was the latest Ebola patient.

With that said, Cedrick stood in the parking lot alone watching his sister walk off.

Chapter - 12

"Damn, girl, what's up wit' the work?" NaNa asked.

"I'm on it," Nessa said, speaking into her phone as she drove.

"Shit, girl, these niggas are thirsty. That shit was so fuckin' good it's got muthafuckas blowin' up my phone. We're missin' money, Nessa."

"I know. Some shit came up I didn't see coming."

"Nessa, I feel you. But not only are we missing money, the pups gotta be paid. I told 'em I would have some money for 'em soon. Niggas don't work for free, young meat. When muthafuckas ain't paid, they start gettin' disgruntled and shit."

"I'm on it now, NaNa. By tomorrow morning I'll have some more work to you, and money."

"A'ight. And remember our conversation about my money. I need that," he added with disdain.

Nessa hated how greedy NaNa had become.

"You've told me enough times," she added just before the two ended their call.

"Shit," Nessa said as she worked the steering wheel. She hated missing out on money. "Fuck!"

The sun was dropping as Nessa made her way to Chavez's mansion. She was feeling queasy though. Sickness from her pregnancy was once again kicking in at the wrong time. She'd eaten some Chinese food earlier and now it was on the verge of coming back up. Realizing she wasn't going to be able to hold it down too much longer, she pulled into a gas station, parked and darted to the bathroom. Rushing inside, she threw up in the toilet until she was dry heaving. Breathing hard, she remained kneeling for a while until she was sure she was done. Minutes later, after cleaning herself up, she headed outside. Heading to her car, rage built up in her when she saw who was leaning against her hood...

Brandon.

"You've got a lot of fucking nerve showing your face," she spewed as she headed towards him.

"Fuck that," he spewed back. "Your ass was getting too big for your damn draws. You needed a reality check."

"Fuck you." She headed around him to the driver's door.

Grabbing her arm, he asked, "Where the fuck are you going?"

Snatching away, she yelled, "Get your hands the fuck off me!"

Grabbing both her wrists, overpowering her and forcefully shoving her back against the car, he placed his face directly in hers and said, "I asked you a Goddamn question, bitch."

"If you don't let me go, Brandon, I'll scream."

Pulling his gun from underneath his suit coat, shoving it underneath her chin, he said, "And I'll blow your muthafucking head all over this damn parking lot."

Nessa's body tensed. She began breathing heavy. She thought for sure the trigger would go off accidentally.

"Now where the fuck are you going?" he asked.

"To get some work from Chavez, Muthafucka. You got all the damn work took, remember, smart ass?"

Keeping a hold of Nessa, he glanced into the car. "Where's the money?"

"What money?"

"Bitch, the money you're buying the work with."

110

"Why?"

"Where is it, damn it!" he yelled, shoving the gun further into her chin.

"I didn't bring it."

"Fuck you mean?"

"Him and I are working out another arrangement."

He stared at her. A sinister smirk then appeared on his face. Realizing what the arrangement was, he said, "A fuckin' whore."

"Fuck you. Don't judge me, nigga."

"First Luke. Then me. Now Chavez." He shook his head. "Don't know why I'm surprised. I knew you wanted to fuck him the first time you met him."

She didn't say anything.

"Well, fuck it. That doesn't concern me, you bitch. What concerns me is the work you'll get. When you get it, call me. We'll meet. I want to see it and count it. Then I'm going with you to drop it off. It's time every player in this organization got an understanding, do you understand? From this point forward, none of you muthafuckas make a move without me knowing about it. If any of you so much as has to take a *shit*, I want to know."

Nessa hated him.

"You got that?" he asked.

She didn't answer him.

Grabbing a handful of hair near her scalp, he snatched her head and asked more sternly, "Do you got that?"

"Yeah."

Letting her go, he walked off. Over his shoulder as he got into his car, he shouted, "And I want to know where that other five hundred thousand is stashed too, bitch!"

Watching him pull off, Nessa was infuriated. When she finally figured out how to get his ass, she was going to make sure it was extreme and painful. She was going to make sure it was terrible enough to make him beg.

Nessa climbed into her car and headed to Chavez's. Finally reaching his mansion, she pulled into the gates, made her way up the drive way and parked beneath the portico. After quickly looking herself over in the overhead mirror, she stepped out of the car. Immediately, she was approached by gunmen. One of them searched her purse and gave it back to her. They then escorted her inside the mansion. Within minutes, she was in what appeared to be a dining room, but larger. The table was long, the length of the room, and lined on both sides with chairs. Expensive porcelain and silverware was set in front of each. Golden chandeliers hung from the high ceilings. Artwork lined the walls. And among it all sitting at the end of the table was Chavez. Behind him, the drapes of the floor to ceiling window were open exposing a gorgeous view of the mansion's grounds.

"Hungry?" Chavez asked as he feasted on shrimp, rice and vegetables.

"No thank you."

"You sure? My cook can prepare whatever you like."

"I'm okay."

Chavez signaled for the men who'd escorted Nessa to leave. They did as they were told. Alone now, Chavez told Nessa after dabbing his mouth with a napkin and taking a sip of wine, "Please have a seat and tell me of your problems."

Nessa made her way alongside the table all the way down to the nearest chair to Chavez. As she did, Chavez pushed his plate aside, pulled out a Cohiba, Cuban cigar, clipped it and lit. He then crossed his legs and focused his eyes on Nessa as she sat down. He listened intently as she told him about the robbery and Brandon's involvement. He also nodded occasionally to let her know he was following her word for word. When she was finished, he said, "Quite a betrayal and quite a problem."

"I have a business to run," she said. "Obviously, this has set me back big time."

"Of course."

"I need help."

"You said on the phone you have no money."

"Everything was tied up in those bricks."

112

"I see."

"I was hoping you and I could work out an arrangement."

Leaning back into his chair with his legs still crossed, he pulled on his Cohiba again and surveyed Nessa's legs from behind the veil of smoke he exhaled. "An arrangement, huh?"

"Yes."

"What sort?" he asked as his eyes arose slowly from her legs to her face making sure to take in all her curves on the way.

"Consignment."

"Consignment, huh?"

"Yes."

Tapping ashes from his cigar into an ashtray, he said, "I'm assuming for the same amount of product you lost?"

"Yes."

"That's a lot of work."

"Yes, but I can get the money back to you quickly. My customers are already lined up for the product."

"Because it's good."

"The best in the state."

"Of course."

Silence.

At least a minute passed.

Finally he spoke, "If I agree to do this, you do understand it would come with stipulations?" he asked.

"Of course," she told him.

"Three to be exact."

She nodded.

"First of all, I will give you twenty bricks. The first stipulation is I expect thirty- five thousand back off of each brick. A total of seven hundred thousand, understood?"

She nodded again.

"The second is, I expect my money in seven days. Not a day late or a penny short. And please understand I am not the light company or insurance company. I don't send bills. If my money is not on the desk of my den in seven days, instead of a notice, I will send killers."

Shivers ran down Nessa's spine with the last sentence he spoke. She stared into his eyes and saw total seriousness, not a hint of humor. Because of that, she knew playing any sort of games with his money would be a foolish move.

"Is that understood?" he asked.

"Yes."

A pause.

Seconds passing.

"And the third?" she asked.

He continued staring into her eyes. His then traveled down her body once again like they'd done earlier. When they made their way back up to hers, he said, "I'm sure you already know."

Nessa understood. And to get those bricks, she was willing to do damn near anything.

"Are the terms understood and accepted?" he asked.

"Yes."

"Splendid."

With that said, he uncrossed his legs, unzipped his slacks and looked directly at Nessa. "I'm a man who always gets what he wants."

Nessa looked past him, pretending to ignore him while hearing every word. She dreaded the moment but knew the sooner she started, the sooner it would be over. "Is that so? Well, I'm a lady that's used to getting whatever she wants, whenever." She added, "And I want those bricks," while sucking her teeth and crossing her arms. She could hear her mother calling her soft and Nessa wanted no parts of being soft.

Nessa stood from her chair, walked over to Chavez, standing between his legs. Chavez had to pry her arms apart, forcefully shoving her on her knees. Nessa stared at his freed his erection. It was smaller than she expected; a *lot* smaller. But of course, she didn't tell him. She simply stuffed it into her mouth and sucked.

Like a king on a throne inflicting his will on a peasant,

Chavez puffed his cigar and looked down at Nessa with a smirk.

Nessa began to make slurping sounds as she devoured Chavez's miniature pole easily. As she did, her nostrils inhaled cologne. She also immediately noticed that he was completely manscaped; absolutely no hair. She sucked hard and deep while caressing and massaging his balls, which were also completely hairless.

"Yessssssss," Chavez moaned as he placed a hand on Nessa's head and began to rub her hair.

Going up and down repeatedly, Nessa went all the way down his shaft to the very base with absolutely no problem. Occasionally, she let the tip escape her mouth so she could run her tongue over the head and across the pee hole.

"You like?" he asked, still rubbing her head like she was a puppy dog.

"Mmm-hmmm," she moaned to him as if she was eating a steak. In reality, sucking his dick was nowhere near as enjoyable as she'd thought when she first met him. The small size was a turn off. But as long as he had the money and cocaine to substitute for the small size of his dick, she would bear it.

"Your mouth is sooooooo hungry," he groaned.

Nessa gave him seductive eyes as she sucked. She even began to fake gagging sounds to stroke his ego. She wanted him to believe she considered his dick a *monster*.

"Feast on it, Nessa. Eat it all."

Nessa gobbled wildly. She could feel him pulsating and throbbing in her mouth.

"Yessssssssss, Nessa, yessssss."

Endless slurping and gagging sounds came from Nessa. They grew louder and louder. They grew more extreme and intense. She sucked like a wild savage. She showed no remorse, no mercy.

Chavez moaned and groaned. His toes curled in his loafers. His teeth gritted. His back stiffened. Nessa's mouth was driving him crazy. Of course he'd had plenty of women on their knees, many exotic and far more beautiful than Nessa. But he

115

had to admit Nessa's mouth was one of the best he'd come across. She was definitely experienced in the art of dick sucking. Knowing she was sending Chavez to the edge, Nessa refused to let him out of her mouth, *period*. She wouldn't even let her mouth rise from the base to the head anymore. She kept him in her throat as if holding his dick hostage. As she did, she made wild gurgling sounds as if he was killing her throat.

"Shittttt!" Chavez yelled.

Nessa kept working feverishly.

Minutes passed.

Chavez couldn't take it anymore. He had to fuck Nessa. Shoving her head back, he stood, swatted his plate and glass crashing to the floor, lifted her up and sat her on the table. Forcing her legs open, he snatched her panties to the side and shoved his dick into her. He then grabbed her and jerked her head back to expose her neck, which he began kissing wildly. She was thankful that her four months of pregnancy still hadn't shown and her washboard abs were still in tact.

"Fuck me, poppy!" Nessa yelled, sounding like she was enjoying it. In reality though, she could barely feel him. She had to squeeze her muscles super tight to get the slightest enjoyment out of it. She knew she wasn't going to get an orgasm but she was definitely going to stroke his ego regardless.

You like Papi's dick?" he asked as he continued kissing her neck.

"I love it, baby. I fucking love it!"

Chavez stroked and shoved his narrow hips. He was all the way in her. His balls were slapping the bottom of her hole.

"Give it to me, Papi!"

Chavez pounded and shoved repeatedly.

"You're so damn big, baby. Oh, God, you're killing me!"

"Take it. Take it, bitch!"

Nessa moaned loudly. The moans weren't real or genuine. She made them sound like they were, though. She made them sound as sincere as possible. "Give it to me, baby!"

Chavez made growling sounds like a beast. He could feel

himself getting ready to pop off. The anticipation and need to make it happen took him over. He went as hard and as deep as he could.

"Give me your cum, Papi. Fill me up!"

Those words fed Chavez's ego. He wanted to give her what she was begging for. He wanted to make her pussy overflow with his cum.

"I need it, Papi. Please, baby, give me all of it!"

Chavez finally exploded with one of the fiercest orgasms he'd had in a long time. Grunts left his mouth as he became limp. .When he was pretty much empty, Nessa rocked her hips back and forth, milking his dick to the last drop causing him to moan. Refusing to let her have anymore of him, he backed away.

The room was now silent.

Turning his back to Nessa while zipping himself up, as if dismissing her, Chavez said, "The bricks will be delivered in a couple hours. The spot will change of course. I'll hit you in a couple hours...I just need a minute alone," he stated with an irritated look on his face.

Nessa climbed off the table and pulled her skirt down.

With his back still to her and now staring out of the window, he reminded her, "Seven days, Nessa. Only seven days. Please, don't make me show you just how ugly I can be."

Understanding, Nessa left the room.

Escorted by several goons, Chetti and Mac made their way through the mansion to Chavez's pool deck. Sitting beside the in-ground pool and underneath a beautiful night sky, he sat at a table staring at a chessboard. He'd played with countless opponents across the planet. But he always found the most enjoyment playing with himself.

"Chavez," Chetti said when she saw him.

Smiling and standing from the table, he opened his arms.

117

"Chetti, so glad you could make it."

The two embraced.

"Please have a seat," he told her. "You haven't aged a bit," he said with a kiss-ass grin.

She sat across from him allowing the chessboard to be between them. Mac stood nearby, chest out…face stern as if he were a match for Chavez's goons.

"I see you still find enjoyment in your favorite pastime," she said, looking at the chessboard.

"Keeps me on my toes."

"Of course."

"A drink?"

"My favorite would be nice."

Chavez signaled for a servant to make her a drink at the nearby wet bar. "Tequila, straight up," he told them.

Chetti grinned.

"I see jail could do nothing to lessen your beauty," he complimented her.

"Not a jail or a situation on earth that can break me down."

He nodded.

The servant handed Chetti her drink. After taking a sip, she looked across the table and said, "So you said you had something to tell me?"

"Yes."

"Well?"

Dressed in Prada trousers, she crossed her legs.

Dressed in a polo styled short sleeve, black Gucci slacks and Ferragamo loafers, he did the same.

"How much do you know about this Nessa girl?"

Chetti wasn't surprised to hear Nessa's name come from Chavez's mouth. In fact, it was just what she wanted to hear. "Enough to know that I don't like the bitch. But for now, she is serving a purpose."

"A purpose?"

"Yes, a purpose. Brandon, did tell you my plan, right?"

118

Chetti was getting pissed.

"Uh, plan? I'm confused."

Mac could see smoke damn near about to come from Chetti's nose and mouth. Her entire disposition had changed.

"So, Brandon told you nothing about how I wanted you to handle Nessa?"

Chavez smiled. He knew Chetti was devious. He knew she was selfish. Those two things were going to lead to Nessa's death. He was sure of it. When fucking with Chetti, the devil wasn't the only heartless muthafucka that wears Prada.

"I haven't seen Brandon since the first day he brought Nessa here."

Chetti's head spun around so quick her neck snapped. "Mac, you kill that muthafucker! No more chances!"

Mac nodded from the corner.

"So?" Chavez asked curiously, "Tell me what Brandon didn't do that you'd like me to do? You know I owe you my life."

Chetti allowed a slight smile to slip from the side of her mouth as she explained how she wanted to benefit from all of Nessa's hard work and grind in the streets. " Every time she makes money, I make more."

"Indeed." Chavez nodded.

"And that fuckin' Luke, when the snitching-ass son of a bitch calls, you let me know. I'm certain he'll try to check in on his little whore."

"Consider it done. But just so you know, he's already called me once to see if Nessa had connected with me. I told him she hadn't."

Chetti grinned wickedly.

She ended with, "So, wait, why did you originally call me here?"

With his legs still crossed, he shifted himself in his seat at an angle, folded his hands and asked, "Telling you this is not in my best interest, but does the name Piper ring a bell to you?"

Chetti's face changed expressions. She hadn't heard that

name in years. "Of course. That was Charles' side bitch."

Chavez began to stroke his goatee with his thumb and forefinger.

"What about her?" Chetti asked.

"What would you say if I told you Nessa and Piper know each other quite intimately?"

Staring intently at him, she asked, "*How* intimately?"

"Very."

Her expression grew extremely serious.

Seconds passed.

"Piper is Nessa's mother," Chavez said.

Chetti couldn't believe what she'd just heard. "You're bullshitting."

He simply looked at her.

"Tell me you're bullshitting me, Chavez."

"Heard it directly from their mouths , Chetti. Both were standing in my den the other day side by side."

Chetti was in a state of disbelief. She was speechless. She could remember taking Charles from Piper. She could remember how scarred Piper was over him leaving her. She remembered it all like it was yesterday. One thing she *didn't* remember though and she was absolutely *sure* he hadn't told her was that she had a daughter.

Chavez said nothing. He simply watched, pleased with himself that he'd shared such valuable information with a colleague he respected.

"That underhanded bitch," Chetti growled. She now knew Nessa's hooking up with Luke hadn't been a coincidence. It had been planned.

Piper and Nessa had been somehow plotting against her.

Without another word said, too infuriated to talk, Chetti stood quickly and stormed off. She couldn't believe that a female would do all of that because their pussy wasn't good enough to keep a man. She wanted Nessa's ass more than ever now.

Chapter-13

The prison infirmary was lined with two dozen beds, each dozen lining the length of two facing walls. Almost everything, including the walls, sheets, and medical machines were white. On one end of the room was a door, where a guard sat outside at a desk. On the opposite end was a window, which was now allowing sun to shine brightly through. The beds were empty except one...

The one Luke was lying in.

Obviously Luke had known the day of his visit with Cedrick something wasn't right. He'd known it as the Sargent walked him back to his cell. And he'd definitely known it when he'd discovered the CO who'd pulled his coattail had either been fired or transferred to another prison the very next day. Luke wasn't sure which. Either way, something wasn't right.

As Luke lay in his bed that night, his mind wandered. What did CO Flippen have to tell him? He'd been a great ally so far, but no one could be trusted. And why did the Sargent feel the need to interrupt him? What was going on? The next morning though, Luke's questions were finally answered. While taking a shower, his back turned to the entrance of the stall, a fellow inmate snuck up behind him and sent a shank through his back. Feeling the sharp pain jolt through his body, Luke turned around quickly, placed his back to the wall and fought hard for his life. Losing blood quickly and knowing he would black out soon, he sustained several cuts from the man's shank before finally being able to grab a hold of him, throw him in a headlock and snap his neck. Finally released, the man's body collapsed to the floor onto his stomach. Blood ran from his mouth into the drain along with the shower's cascading water. Moments later, Luke collapsed also.

Waking up in the infirmary a day later, his stab wound stitched, his cuts bandaged, Luke knew he'd been set up. He knew the Sargent had allowed the inmate into the shower with him. That's what the CO had been trying to tell him. His life was on the line.

Luke now lay on his back staring up at the ceiling. He couldn't sleep. He was absolutely *refusing* to sleep. Every time the doctor or nurse came into the room, he grew nervous. Everything in him and about him went on high alert. His eyes always darted to the door in anticipation of someone coming to finish him off. He knew the attempt on his life wasn't going to be the last.

The door opened. Luke's eyes darted to it.

"Luke!" Pamela called as she was escorted into the infirmary. She quickly ran to his bed and hugged him.

Grimacing with pain, Luke found comfort in Pamela's arms. He hugged her tightly.

"Who did this to you?" she asked, releasing him and quickly letting her eyes worriedly survey his bandages.

"One of the damn inmates. I killed him."

She gasped.

"I had no choice."

"Well, why did he try to kill you?"

Luke didn't answer.

"Goddamn it, Luke!" she yelled. "You're always so fucking secretive. Talk to me!"

Luke still didn't answer. He just avoided eye contact with Pamela.

"Luke, look, I'm not naive. Just because I don't say anything doesn't mean I don't know. I know that you've been in business with some dangerous people. I know that you've done some horrible things. I know it, Luke. The Feds wouldn't be going through so much to convict you and your family if you were the damn Dalai Lama."

He sighed with disappointment.

"I'm not stupid, Luke. I know you have people who would want you killed now that they know you're testifying. Which one of them wants you dead?"

Shaking his head, he said, "Pamela, you don't understand. The less you know, the better off you are."

"Damn it, Luke, don't you see? I'm already a target. I'm your girl. Whoever wants you dead, don't you think they know that already?"

"Pamela…"

"Is it over drugs? Is it over business? Who are they? Maybe I can pay them off."

Luke honestly didn't know who was exactly behind the hit on his life. It could've been Chetti. It could've been Brandon. It could've been some of the people the family had done business with out of fear that he would roll over on them just like he was planning on doing to Chetti. He knew word was out that he was snitching.

Pamela calmed herself down. "Baby, I did some research."

"What do you mean?"

Looking uneasy, she said, "I wasn't trying to spy on you or anything. I just wanted to know more about the case so I looked into it carefully, especially the stuff regarding your mother. Luke, some of the stuff I saw terrified me."

She walked away from the bed and headed to the window. Staring out, she said, "Murder, kidnapping, extortion; she's heartless."

He stared at her back.

"But what scared me most was the fact that although I

love you, Luke, I know the apple doesn't fall too far from the tree."

"What are you saying, Pamela?"

Turning to him and looking him directly in the eyes, she asked, "How much of that were you yourself involved in?"

He didn't utter a word. He was starting to become suspicious of Pamela's motives. First, it was her knowing about Darien's death before he caught wind of it and now this.

With a tear beginning to stream down her face, she asked, "How many men did you kill, Luke? How many did you kidnap?"

"Pamela!"

"Tell me!" she screamed angrily.

"I can't do that."

"Then how the Hell am I supposed to know who may possibly come after me because of my connection to you?"

"Pamela, I would never put you in harm's way."

"Luke, I'm guilty by association."

The room went silent.

Moments went by.

"Talk to me, Luke. Let me in, please."

Luke wanted so badly to open up to Pamela. He wanted to confess to her like a sinner to a priest. He was truly beginning to realize she loved him and was on his side. Still though, he just couldn't. He couldn't tell her the secrets she wanted to hear.

"I can't, Pamela. I'm sorry but I can't."

Shaking her head and wiping her tears away, she said, "Baby, I love you but you're making it hard for me to *stay* in love with you."

The two stared at each other.

A full minute passed.

Finally, Pamela told him, "I've got a meeting to get to. I've got to go." She then headed for the door.

Luke wanted to call out for her realizing she hadn't kissed him before ending the visit. He knew she was hurting. He knew she felt somewhat betrayed. Sighing, he opened his mouth to call her but not a word came out. A moment later, he could only watch her back as she walked out and headed down the hall.

◯◈◈

Trinity sat at the living room table staring at the cell phone in front of her. Along with it, she stared at the gun beside it. In her mind, she couldn't get the images of her father's murder to stop playing over and over. She could see and smell the blood spilling from his throat soiling his chest. She could see his eyes widening as the blade of the knife sliced from one end of his throat to the other. She could hear the gurgling sounds coming from his mouth. It was all so sickening and heartbreaking. She couldn't even sleep behind it.

Trinity wanted Nessa's head on a platter. She wanted to do to her what she'd done to her father. She wanted to see her blood spill. Everything inside Trinity yearned for it like food, water and air. She now had just as much hatred in her heart for Nessa as she had for Chetti. Up until she'd seen that video, she'd thought that was impossible.

Grabbing the phone, Trinity dialed Nessa's number. Placing the phone to her ear and listening to it ring three times, she once again saw the brutal images of her father dying in her head.

"Yeah," Nessa's voice said answering the call.

"Nessa?" Trinity asked.

"Yeah, who's this?"

"Trinity."

With excitement in her voice, Nessa almost yelled, "Trinity, is this really you?"

"It's me."

"Girl, I thought you were dead. I thought Chetti had done something to you."

"Why would you think that?"

"Because of what I found out. She thought I was going to tell you."

"What did you find out?"

125

"We need to talk."

"Can you meet with me today?"

"Yes."

The two set up a meeting place and ended their call. Afterward, once again Trinity sat there in silence. This time though, she took the gun into her hands and held the grip tightly. Wanting revenge, she placed her finger around the trigger and anticipated what it would be like to squeeze off a shot directly into Nessa's face. However it would feel, she was about to find out.

Music played at a low volume from hidden overhanging speakers as Trinity walked into the sports bar. She saw Nessa sitting on a stool at the far end of the bar and headed towards her.

Seeing Trinity, Nessa immediately stood and hugged her. "God, I swear I thought she'd killed you."

Trinity grew almost nauseous at the feel of Nessa's murdering arms around her. It took everything inside her to hug Nessa back.

Both ladies finally sat down.

Trinity ordered a drink.

Because of the pregnancy, Nessa didn't. Instead, she drank a glass of Ginger Ale.

"Where have you been?" Nessa asked.

Trinity wanted to slap Nessa off her stool, but fought through it. Every moment was a struggle. "Had to lay low for a while," she said. "Everything's been so hectic lately."

"Shit, you got that right."

"Can't trust anyone."

"What do you mean?"

"My own fuckin' mom tried to have me killed."

"Trinity, about that, I never meant for that to happen. I just thought you should know."

"Know what?"

"About Cedrick?"

"Cedrick?"

"Yeah."

"What about him?"

Nessa looked at Trinity with disbelief. "You don't know?"

Of course Trinity knew. She just wanted to keep Nessa as much off guard as possible. "Know what?"

Nessa paused.

"Well?"

"Trinity, Cedrick, is alive."

"What are you talking about?"

"Trinity, I saw him with my own two eyes. He was in one of the rooms of the mansion. Chetti was holding him there against his will. Luke knew about it. And I'm sure Darien knew about it."

Acting dismayed, Trinity said, "Nessa, don't play with me like that."

"Trinity, I would never play those types of games. I would never lie about something like that."

Lying, hypocritical bitch, Trinity thought to herself. The bitch had the nerve to look her in the face and pretend they were cool when she knew she'd murdered her father. Now she's talking about she would never play *those* types of games? Trinity wanted to reach in her purse at that moment, grab the gun and blow her face off. If the bar had been empty, no witnesses, no doubt she would've.

"I...I...I," Trinity stuttered, acting like she was speechless.

"I know it's crazy, Trinity. But I swear on everything I love, I saw him."

"Then where is he?"

"I don't know."

Trinity sat in silence as in deep thought. Then slamming her fist on the table, she said through gritted teeth, "Those evil

127

bastards," speaking of her family. "Those muthafuckas."

"I'm sorry."

"They wanted his power. They wanted to run the family." A ferocious anger was all over her face.

"We can get them back, Trinity."

"What do you mean?"

"I've been making moves out here since I got out. In all honesty, your brother Luke tried to cross me. I had no choice but to do what I had to do to survive."

Nessa went into detail about everything that had transpired since she'd gotten out of jail including the fact that Chetti wanted her dead and the fact that Brandon had been acting ridiculous lately. She brought Trinity completely up to date.

"I could definitely use you on my team," she said. "There are not too many people I can trust. Right now me and my squad are working with twenty bricks. They'll definitely be gone by the end of the week. From there, we re-up and keep building. Trinity, we can easily be larger than Chetti, Luke and Darien *ever* were."

Trinity acted as if she was giving it consideration. She thought about what the agents had told her and asked of her. She thought about her own revenge. It all weighed on her mind.

"This can be the best way to find your brother," Nessa added.

Hearing that, Trinity realized this was all perfect. This was a way for her to get Nessa, Nessa's mother, Chetti, Brandon and Luke all in one net together. All of their dislike and distrust for each other could work in Trinity's favor. She had a hatred for *all* of them, and since Agent Logan had already told her the good news about Darien's death, she felt good about knocking the rest of them off one by one.

"You're right, Nessa. I'm in."

Trinity figured by being underneath Nessa, if she played her cards right, not only could she walk away with revenge...

She could walk away with everything.

Chapter-14

Piper headed up the walkway nearly stomping the concrete like it had done something wrong to her. Bitterness and fury was evident on her face. Her mouth was in a snarl. Her eye brows were arched angrily. Her breathing was fast, causing her breasts to heave forward and backward underneath her shirt quickly. Over her shoulder was the strap of a very large purse, which she was gripping tightly. Reaching the steps of the one-storied home, she stomped up each of them, walked across the porch, snatched open the screen door and began pounding hard on the front door. Unsatisfied with just banging on the door, she began repeatedly pressing the doorbell. As she did, she gripped the strap of her purse even tighter than before needing to be near what she had stuffed inside it. It didn't take but a few seconds for the front door to come flying open.

"Piper, what the fuck is wrong with you?!" Brandon yelled, standing in the doorway.

"Don't ask stupid questions!" she yelled back. "You know what the fuck is wrong with me. What the fuck is wrong with *your* ass?!"

Snatching her by the arm, he pulled her inside.

"Get the fuck off me, Brandon!"

He held a tight grip on her arm until the door was

slammed shut. Finally letting her go, he screamed, "Are you fucking crazy? You don't come to my damn house drawing attention like that. I've got neighbors!"

"Fuck your damn neighbors!" she screamed back at him, tossing her purse to the couch.

"Piper…"

"Don't "*Piper*" me, muthafucka. What the fuck is wrong with you? Are you trying to destroy everything!"

"Fuck you talking about?"

"You dumb muthafucka, Londo, rolled up on Nessa to recoup the 50 grand that your snake ass never gave them! Instead they took all the product she'd just gotten from Chavez! Now we've *all* lost money!"

He shrugged his shoulders followed by a, "So".

"So? That's all you can say, bitch!"

"As fast as the coke has been moving, the money lost will be made up in no time!"

"Brandon, you're tripping!"

"No, Nessa's tripping. The bitch was beginning to get it in her head that she was running shit. That's why I never gave them the fifty grand! She didn't even want to tell me where the money was stashed. I wouldn't have known Sidra had it if I hadn't demanded Nessa take me to it the other night after she got the latest work from Chavez!"

"You're paranoid!"

"Oh, *I'm* paranoid, huh?"

"Yes!"

"What about you? You don't trust the bitch enough to even tell her you and me know each other, remember?"

Piper didn't answer.

"You wanted me to keep it quiet so I could watch the bitch because you wanted to be sure she wasn't making moves behind *your* damn back, remember?"

Piper could only stand there seething. She knew he was right. She couldn't dispute the truth.

"Yeah," he said, seeing she couldn't respond. "Just like

you don't trust the bitch no farther than you can throw her, I don't neither. I had to knock her down a couple notches."

"So, you jeopardize our whole shit?"

"It was never jeopardized. We still had the other five hundred stashed."

"It was never jeopardized, huh?" Piper knew Sidra was keeping the money but Brandon had no idea.

"No."

"So, you being coked the fuck up all the fuckin' time isn't jeopardizing it?"

"What are you talking about?"

"Don't play stupid. Nessa said you're snorting more cocaine around here than Tony Montana!"

"Look, I do just a little every now and then. It's no different than your smoking and drinking. Besides, what I do on my own time is my business."

"Your own time?" she asked in disbelief. "She said you're high as a kite damn near every time she sees you lately. That's not your *own* time. Muthafucka, that's *our* time. You're jeopardizing all of us with that stupid shit!"

Beginning to pace the floor, she said, "Fuckin' idiot. Goddamn idiot. This is what happens when I fuck with *idiots.*"

"Watch your damn mouth, Piper."

Turning towards him, she rushed into his face and screamed as loud as she could, "Idiot, idiot, idiot. Oh, did I forget to tell you you're a muthafuckin' *idiot*?"

"Piper, I'm warning you!" he screamed back. "Watch how you talk to me!"

"Fuck you!"

"Keep on bitch, I'll smoke your ass the same way I did your late husband, Byron."

Piper froze. His words marinated in her head. Smoked Byron? *Not that she liked the son of a bitch or anything, but who was he to think he could go around killing people; especially Nessa's father? Oh, so, that's why Nessa kept talking crazy about her dad. Bitch still sneaky. She would probably never tell*

131

me about that, stupid ho.

Breathing heavily through her nose, Piper walked up closer to Brandon. "Let's see you smoke me, muthafucka!"

Losing control, Brandon let loose with a backhand so swift and with so much force it spun Piper around and sent her clear across the room to the floor. "Bitch, I said watch your mouth!"

Lying on the floor, Piper was dazed heavily. She placed her hand to her mouth and saw not only double, but blood also.

"Bitch, I'm equal partner in this thing!" he yelled. "I hooked you bitches up with the plug. I keep the local authorities off your ass so you could operate. I'm the one taking a chance on losing my job and going to prison if I get caught!"

Piper grew infuriated. She'd never been hit by a man before. Seeing red, she got to her feet and charged directly at Brandon so fast he had no time to react. When she collided with him, both he and her went flying over a cocktail table and knocked over a lamp. With him now lying on his back, she rose up and began raining fists down on him.

"Piper!" he yelled, trying to block her strikes.

"You muthafucka!" she screamed as she kept throwing punches.

"Piper!"

"You hit me, son of a bitch? You hit me?!"

"Piper, stop!"

Piper kept on raining punches.

"Piper, get your crazy ass off me!"

"Fuck you!"

More punches.

More yelling.

Brandon was finally able to grab hold of Piper's arms. Holding them, he developed enough force to get her off him and on her back. He straddled her chest and pinned her wrists to the floor.

"Get the fuck off me, Brandon!"

"No!"

Blood was trickling from Brandon's nose. His bottom lip was split. His left eye was red.

"Get off me!"

"Not until you calm your crazy ass down!"

"Brandon, get off!"

"No, Piper!"

Suddenly, Piper let out an ear piercing scream.

"Bitch, what the Hell is wrong with you?" He yelled, placing a hand over her mouth. She bit him, causing him to snatch his hand away quickly like he'd just touched the handle of a hot pot. "Goddamn it!" he yelled in pain while shaking his hand.

"Get off me now, Brandon!" she screamed as she clawed at his face with her free hand.

"Owwwwww, bitch!" he yelled in pain as her nails collected skin from his face. He quickly grabbed her wrist again and slammed it to the floor.

"I hate you, Brandon. I should've never brought you in on this shit!"

"Well, I'm in now. I've invested just as much as everybody else. And from here on out, every last one of you bitches are going to respect me. From now on, no moves are made without me being in on 'em!"

Piper began coughing.

"Do you understand me?" he asked.

Piper continued coughing again. As she did, the coughing grew heavier. Before long, it turned into a severe coughing fit.

Growing worried, Brandon asked, "Piper, are you okay?"

Suddenly, by accident, she coughed blood into Brandon's face. "What the fuck?" he gasped.

"Get off me."

Brandon climbed off her. "What the Hell, Piper?"

Ignoring him and still coughing, Piper grabbed her purse from the couch and quickly headed down the hall to the bathroom. Reaching the bathroom and shutting the door, she turned on the faucet, grabbed a wash rag and began cleaning herself up.

In the living room, still surprised at what had just happened, feeling the blood on his face and looking down to see it on his shirt, Brandon quickly took off his shirt, tossed it and headed to the kitchen in a wife beater. Going directly to the kitchen sink and turning on the faucet, he began cleaning away the blood.

The doorbell rang.

"Shit," he said.

The doorbell rang again.

Turning off the water and drying his face with a dish towel, he went back to the living room and opened the door to see Londo and one of his henchmen standing on the porch. His henchman was holding a leopard print book bag.

Looking over Brandon's shoulder and seeing a broken lamp and the cocktail table flipped, Londo asked, "You forgot we were coming, homes?"

"No, no," Brandon said quickly.

"You sure?"

"Yeah, you're good."

Londo and his boy looked at Brandon skeptically.

"Everything's good. Come in."

The Mexicans walked inside. Brandon shut the door behind them. "A beer or anything?" he offered.

"Nah, holmes, just want to get this shit over with and go. A deal is a deal, hombre."

"Alright."

"Been throwing a party or something, holmes?" Londo's goon asked Brandon while looking at the overturned table.

"Something like that," Brandon told him as he turned the table upright again.

The henchman handed Brandon the book bag. Unzipping it, Brandon saw some of the bricks of cocaine taken from Nessa.

"Half the load we stole from your girl," one of the men stated.

He nodded approvingly then looked back toward the

134

bathroom.

In the bathroom, Piper was still cleaning herself up when she'd heard the doorbell ring. After shutting off the water and wiping away blood, she could hear voices outside in the living room as she looked at her reflection in the mirror. Wanting to know what was going on, she headed to the door and placed her ear to it. Listening, she could hear what sounded like Mexican men with strong west coast accents. She listened carefully. Unable to hear clearly, she softly turned the doorknob and opened the door slowly. Peeking out, she saw two Mexican men in Dickies, Cortez Nikes, and light jackets. Over their eyes they wore dark Locs.

Piper ducked back down, just as she saw Brandon's head turn in her direction.

"Hey, you guys sure you don't want a drink?" he asked the Mexicans, attempting to get them to the kitchen and out of ear shot of the bathroom. "Come in the kitchen. I got some beer in the fridge."

"Nahhh, homie," Londo said firmly. "We're good. Don't want no drinks."

"You sure? Come on. A cold beer over business."

"No beer. No drinks. Let's get down to business."

Brandon grew nervous. He knew Piper was going to come out of the bathroom at any second. The last thing he wanted was for her to hear what was about to be discussed. She was a firecracker waiting to blast off.

"Now, we held up our end of the deal," Londo rambled. "We robbed your girl and split the bricks with you. You held up half your end by getting the Bishops out of the way. Now it's time for you to hold up the other half. When do we hook up with Chavez?"

"Huh?" Brandon asked nervously. With Piper on his mind, he honestly hadn't heard the question just asked of him.

"Chavez, holmes," the goon said. "When do we hook up with him?"

"Uhhhhhhh…"

They both looked at Brandon skeptically.

Londo had a suspicious look when he asked, "Yo, you good? You look like you're on some preoccupied shit."

Glancing back at the bathroom again, Brandon said, "No, everything's cool."

Glancing at his partner, Londo asked Brandon, "Why do you keep looking back, holmes?"

"Huh?"

"Stop with the fuckin' "*huhs*", holmes!" the goon yelled angrily. "Why the hell do you keep looking back?"

"No reason."

"Yo, something's not right. You actin' real nervous and shit."

"Nahhhhh, everything's cool."

The goon pulled out his gun. Londo did the same.

Quickly throwing up his hands while still holding the bag, Brandon said, "Fellas, you're over reacting."

"Fuck you, holmes!"

"Fellas…"

"What's back there? Why do you keep looking back?"

"Nothing."

"Go check it out," Londo told his goon.

In the bathroom, what Piper had heard shocked her. The Mexicans hadn't robbed Nessa because Brandon *didn't* pay. They robbed her because he *did* pay. He'd paid them to rob her. As payment, they kept half the bricks and gave Brandon the other half. That wasn't all, though. Brandon had been working against the Bishops all along. Under a deal he'd cut with the Mexicans, he promised he could get the Bishops out of the way, which obviously he did. Now he and the Mexicans could have free rein over the Bishop's territory with him keeping the local cops off their ass. Also included in the deal was Brandon's promise to now hook them up with Chavez.

The goon was now headed towards the bathroom door.

Pissed, Piper could care less about Brandon crossing Chetti, Luke and Darien. What had her pissed off was the fact

136

that he'd crossed her and Nessa. No wonder he wasn't stressing about the amount of work she'd gotten robbed for. The son of a bitch was getting half of it back for himself.

"Muthafucka," she said. "That snake ass lying mutha-fucka."

The goon was getting closer.

She stood there for a moment. More than anger pulsated throughout her. More than anger flowed through her veins. She'd been betrayed. She knew Brandon had no intentions of sharing the bricks. He was trying to fuck her over just as well as Nessa.

"Son of a bitch."

Piper looked at her purse sitting on the toilet. Quickly, she walked to it, reached inside and pulled out a .45 Revolver that resembled the one from the old school Clint Eastwood Dirty Harry movies. Holding it in her hand, fully loaded it felt heavy. She didn't care though. Despite its size, she could handle it.

Piper was in no way, shape or form going to let Brandon get away with what he had done. She also was for damn sure not going to let the Mexicans move in on what was supposed to be hers. Refusing to let any of that happen, she clicked the hammer back on the gun, grabbed the doorknob knowing the gunman was nearly right outside. Closing her eyes and breathing hard, she swallowed a lump in her throat. Now ready, she snatched open the door, gripped the handle of the gun with both hands and raised it in time to surprise the goon.

BOOM!!!!!
BOOM!!!!!

Piper let off two shots. One ripped half the man's skull off. Blood and brain splattered everywhere. The other bullet tore half his neck off. He fell to the floor backwards with his arms outstretched. He was dead immediately.

"Bitch!" Londo shouted. He then let off two shots from his Glock, intended to blast Piper.

Falling sideways against the wall to dodge the bullets, Piper let off three shots of her own. All three hit Londo directly in the chest, blew his heart out his back and lifted him clear off the floor. The force tossed him backwards to the couch where he landed in a sitting position. With three huge holes in his chest and blood pouring heavily from them, he slumped over dead.

"What the fuck are you doing!" Brandon yelled, his chest heaving up and down.

Walking towards him, Piper said, "You low down mutha-fucka."

With the book bag in his right hand, he held his free hand in front of him as if it could possibly stop a bullet.

Tears flowed from Piper's face, yet no fear was in her eyes.

He said quickly, "Piper, it's not what it looks like."

"The fuck it ain't!"

"Piper, I was going to split the work with you. I swear to God."

Piper continued to head towards him with the gun aimed.

"I swear, Piper," he said as he took a step back.

"Drop the bag, Brandon."

"Piper, I…"

"Drop the fucking bag, nigga!" she roared.

"Okay, okay," he said quickly. He dropped the bag.

"Turn around."

"Piper, look, I…"

"Turn!!!!!"

He did as he was told.

"Get on your knees."

"Piper…"

"Now!!!!!"

He did.

Piper stepped up behind him and placed the gun to his skull. "You fuckin' snake. You fucked and betrayed both me and my daughter. And you killed Byron. Nothing about you is right!"

"Now, Piper, think about this. Think about what you're doing. I'm a federal agent. You kill me, the agency will rain hell down on you. I'm serious. Do you know what they do to people who kill Feds? They'll fry you, Piper. And if they ever discover a way to bring people back from the dead, they'll bring you back and fry you again. Think about that, Piper. Don't do this."

Piper kept the gun aimed.

"Okay, okay, baby, I'm sorry I crossed you. Piper, look, we can work this out. We can split the bricks, sweetheart. Shit, as a matter of fact, I don't even want them. You can have them. Take them, baby. I don't want them."

Piper said not a word. She just kept her eyes and the gun aimed at the center of his skull.

Growing frustrated that his words weren't working, he yelled, "Goddamn it, Piper!" Tears began to stream down his face. "Please don't kill me. I don't want to die, Piper. Please let me live. I'll get out of town. I promise!"

Knowing he was lying, Piper finally did what she knew had no choice but to do...

She squeezed the trigger.

As the thundering sound of the gun shot rattled the room, Brandon's head exploded like a pumpkin. The power of the gun and bullet sent blood splatter back into Piper's face. As it did, she watched Brandon's body collapse to the floor. Seconds after he fell, knowing she had no time to stick around, she snatched the book bag and darted out the back door. As she did, she began coughing heavily again. Even in such an extreme situation, her cancer was showing no mercy.

Piper's days were numbered.

Chapter-15

Bishop funerals were usually lavish and extravagant events. They usually took place in cathedrals. There were usually hundreds to thousands of people in attendance, all dressed in the most expensive clothes. There were usually Limos and Bentleys lining the curb and stretching from one end of the street to the other. Every Bishop was sent out that way; like kings and queens.

Not Darien, though.

Darien's funeral took place in the tiny chapel of The County Jail. Although dead, the Feds were not going to release him from state custody until their case against him was over. Even then, if found guilty and convicted, his body would remain in Potter's Field with a wooden steak for a head stone until his entire sentence was up. Then and *only* then would his family be able to have his body dug up and transported to the burial place of their choosing if they hadn't forgotten about him by then.

Chetti was sitting in the front row of the chapel along with Mac as the pastor spoke from the podium beside Darien's closed casket. After Darien's body had been with mortuary services for longer than three weeks there was no way he could have an open casket funeral.

There were only several other people in the chapel. Usually, a Bishop funeral was a guaranteed packed house. But now since the money had dried up, family was showing they weren't truly family at all. Mortgages, college tuitions and everything else the family needed depended on Chetti, Luke and Darien to provide. Nothing could any longer be paid for, as loyalty was a thing of the past. Darien was now considered out of sight and out of mind.

Chetti wasn't sure if Luke would attend. She doubted it. He'd probably either viewed the body *before* the official funeral, or he would view it *afterward*. She knew the Feds wouldn't bring him knowing he was a snitch, and that his life was on the line because of it. Neither Trinity nor Cedrick showed up either. And just like Luke, Chetti wasn't expecting them to although she still had Mac out looking for the two of them every day. She *was* surprised though that Brandon hadn't shown up. In fact, he hadn't answered his phone in a few days. Chetti was definitely displeased with that.

As the pastor spoke, Chetti sat in a black Dolce & Gabanna dress. A dark veil hung over her face from her fedora. Her legs were crossed. Her shoulders were straight. She held her head high. Still though, underneath the concealment of the fedora, tears were running down her cheeks.

The door of the chapel opened. A young lady entered. Chetti turned to see her and was surprised that she'd shown. The young lady was her niece Raquel, the niece who was having sex with Darien the day the mansion was busted. Chetti wasn't expecting to see her but was glad she was coming to show her respects.

Reaching the front row of the chapel, the opposite row Chetti was sitting in, Raquel sat down. She then looked over at Chetti. Chetti looked over at her also. Expecting to see sadness, Chetti was a little thrown off guard when she saw Raquel looking at her with a stone-like glare. She couldn't quite make out what was behind it. All she knew was it wasn't the type of expression people usually wear during a funeral. Shrugging it off, Chetti placed her attention back on the pastor.

Twenty minutes passed.

Finally, he asked, "Does the family have any final request?"

Chetti stood from her chair. Mac was beside her. Dramatically, she made her way to the casket like Jackie Onassis on her way to President Kennedy's casket. She moved slowly and in a rhythm purposely designed to keep all eyes on her. As usual, even during a funeral, she had to be the center of attention. Reaching the casket, she looked at the photo of her son that sat on top of the casket. She rubbed her finger across the photo, touching his cheek. Her heart broke immediately.

Chetti never had remorse for having someone killed. She'd had more men and women killed than she could count or remember. It was what she had to do to hold onto her power. If she didn't, she herself would've been murdered a long time ago. But having Darien killed still haunted her. She loved him. She loved him more than Luke and definitely more than Trinity, and would have no remorse once she had them killed. But Darien…he truly was her heart. Feeling her knees get weak, she collapsed onto the casket.

"Darien!" she screamed. "Darien, come back to me!"

The few in attendance took Chetti's actions as being a performance. She had always been dramatic. Even Raquel pursed her lips to the side. Everyone knew Chetti was a cold-hearted bitch incapable of caring or loving anyone but herself.

"My baby!" she hollered with tears streaming down her face. Her pain and actions were genuine. Fuck what everyone else thought. She loved her son. She loved him tremendously.

Mac grabbed a hold of his boss and pulled her into his arms. She placed the side of her face against his chest and began to cry all over his suit. As she did, he escorted her back to her chair.

Raquel was the next to stand and make her way to the casket. Reaching it, she rubbed her hand across Darien's casket. For moments, she just stared at the casket, then she looked back at Chetti. No words left her mouth. No tears fell from her eyes.

143

She just stood there in total silence. Then, Raquel hocked up a huge glob of saliva and spit on the casket.

Gasps filled the room.

The pastor looked at her in surprise.

"You rapist!" Raquel screamed! "You fuckin' rapist! You and your crazy-ass mother!"

Chattering filled the room.

Raquel turned around and faced Chetti. "You evil bitch," she snarled. "You stood by and watched him rape me!"

Chetti was caught off guard. She didn't quite know how to respond. At the moment, she was truly grief stricken.

Stepping towards Chetti, Raquel yelled, "You dirty bitch. You let that bastard rape me!"

"Nonsense," Chetti finally responded. "You're delirious."

"Delirious, my ass. You drugged me and let that nigga rape me!"

Raquel charged at Chetti.

Mac stood and immediately got in between the two ladies. He then grabbed Raquel.

"Get off me!" she screamed. "Get the fuck off me!"

Mac kept a hold of her.

Wiping away her tears, stiffening her posture and crossing her legs, Chetti's moment of grief disappeared. She went back to her old self. Looking at Raquel from behind her veil, she said, "Why would my son rape you? He had women swooning at his feet. He'd never give a homely looking wench like you the time of day."

Raquel kicked harder. "Let me go!" she yelled as she scratched and kicked. "Let me go!"

Officers rushed into the chapel. Quickly, they reached Raquel. Having to force her to the floor, place her hands behind her back, and slap the cuffs on her wrists, they finally got her back to her feet and began dragging her, fighting, towards the door.

"Chetti, you're a dead bitch!" she screamed. "I swear to

God, you're a dead bitch!"

Sitting rigid in her chair and staring straight ahead, never once turning to watch Raquel being dragged out, Chetti sat there with a smirk. She had no worries, no cares. Many people had threatened her over the years. But that was all their words were though...threats.

No one had the balls to touch her.

"You're dead, Chetti. You're dead, you evil bitch. I swear to God, as soon as I have this baby, I'm going to kill you!"

Chetti heard Raquel loud and clear but didn't move an inch. She said not a word. With no worries, she sat next to Mac as the threats grew more and more distant. Eventually, they silenced. When they did, all that was on her mind was joy. Although Darien had gone on to burn in hell, he'd at least kept the bloodline pure. Now he just had to find a way to get custody of her grandbaby the moment Raquel gave birth.

Nessa was surprised to receive a call from Chavez early that morning. Immediately she thought he was calling her concerning their deal. So far, the bricks were moving quickly as expected. "Everything's going fine, Chavez," she told him just after answering the phone. "Your money will be on time."

"That's great to hear," he said. "But, that's not why I'm calling."

"What's up?"

"Would you like to go out for lunch? I have something I want to discuss with you."

Nessa accepted.

"Will send a limo for you," he told her.

She smiled widely. He'd never done that before.

"Well, sounds good to me," she stated just before the two ended their call.

An hour later, Nessa found herself in the backseat of a

white, fully loaded Bentley. Expecting to head back to Chavez's
mansion, she was surprised when the Bentley took her to the air-
port and pulled up near a private luxury jet. Seeing Chavez
standing at its steps caused Nessa's insides to moisten. The
chauffeur then hopped out of the Bentley, headed to Nessa's
door and opened it. She emerged wearing a black Prada dress
and Prada sunshades straight off the fashion runway. She looked
stunning.

As she strutted across the runway to meet Chavez he
smiled.

"You look beautiful," he complimented her.

"Thank you."

The two then walked up the jet's steps and went inside.
Nessa wasted no time in asking, "Where are we headed?"

"No questions , please. Just enjoy," he said, kissing her
hand.

What Chavez didn't know was that Nessa was no longer
the coy young women that he'd started doing business with over
a month ago. She was maturing, learning the game, and becoming a real boss. She knew not to trust anyone, not even Chavez.

"Is this in my best interest?" she asked.

"Of course," he responded then signaled for the pilot to
prepare for take-off.

Minutes later, they were thirty thousand feet in the air. A
few hours later, they were touching down in Beverly Hills
where they were picked up by a limo and driven to a five-star
restaurant on Rodeo Drive. Once inside, Nessa noticed that
everyone seemed to know Chavez. It was obvious he visited
often. The two were escorted to a table.

"Order anything you want," Chavez told her.

Opening the menu, Nessa saw that there was not a single
meal for less than two hundred dollars. Her eyes were set on the
Masa Toro rolls, and the Wagyu aged primed rib. Before long,
they both ordered their meals and began to converse. Around
them sitting at other tables were attorneys, doctors, CEOs and
other high priced members of Beverly Hills society. With them

sat beautiful women, mostly young, with diamonds around their necks and name brands on their backs.

"I have a question for you?" Chavez asked as he sipped from a glass of rare champagne.

"What is it?"

"How long do you think you can hustle in the streets?"

"What do you mean?"

"I mean that headed in the direction you're going, it's only a matter of time before you're caught. Don't get me wrong. I commend you for reaching the level you have. But, Nessa, the higher you climb, the greater the stakes."

"I'm doing what I have to do."

"I understand. But the way you're going, I see the Feds in your future, the IRS, the DEA."

Nessa listened intently.

"You can't truly rise in this game without security. I'm talking judges, prosecutors, Federal Agents, DEA Agents, connections in government. I'm talking powerful alliances, people who can keep the law off your back."

Nessa was truly interested. She knew she needed the big wigs behind her as she climbed the ladder to success.

"I can give you those things, Nessa."

"And what do I have to do to get those things? I know you're not offering them for free."

"I'm looking to expand into Baltimore and New York. And obviously I know you're looking to grow also. I need someone willing to be my representation in those two cities. I'll provide you with the product, Nessa. All you have to do is build the clientele."

Leaning forward and folding his hands on the tabletop, he said, "Nessa, I'm interested in you. I have been since the first day I laid eyes on you. I like your style. I like your beauty. I like everything about you, but specifically your hustle. I like the way you get out and get it. This could definitely be a great opportunity for you."

Nessa was definitely giving the offer deep thought.

147

"You accept, I'll provide my product to you at rock bottom prices and on credit. I'll also provide those connections that I spoke about."

Unfolding his hands and taking hers while looking directly into her eyes, he said, "I like you. I'm interested in you."

Nessa stared into his eyes. She could see that he wanted more from her than just a business relationship.

"You can rise to the top of this game, Nessa. You can be the most powerful woman the game has ever seen. I can give that to you."

It didn't take long for Nessa to accept. There was no way she could turn it down. Since Chavez had the best cocaine she'd ever come across, she knew the Baltimore streets and the New York streets would love it. It wouldn't take long for her to build clientele. She'd then have both cities along with Washington D.C under her belt. From there, she'd possibly expand to another city.

Thankful that she'd accepted, Chavez said, "Great, we have to celebrate."

The two celebrated by spending money, specifically Chavez. He took Nessa on a shopping spree that dwarfed any and every spree Luke had ever taken her on. Buying her Gucci, Chanel, Prada, Versace and more, he'd spent ninety grand on her in less than an hour.

Finally, back on the private jet, the two spoke more about the deal while enjoying a glass of fine wine and lavishly prepared meal. Their conversation soon turned into another fuck session. Nessa couldn't believe his little dick was turning her on, so she figured it had to be the money or her raging hormones. She was definitely showing slightly, hoping Chavez still couldn't tell.

While finger fucking her on the plush leather seats then quickly fucking her from behind, Chavez called out, "You're fucking me well, Mami, giving me all this pussy. What am I going to do with you?" He smacked her ass, flipped her over and pushed her off the seat. Turning to walk away, he made

Nessa beg for it, "Papi, don't leave me. Please bring that dick back over here."

When he walked back with a shit eating grin on his face, Nessa knew what that meant. Chavez loved having his ass eaten out more than having his dick sucked. Nessa obliged and went to work on his shaven hole with her thick pink tongue. Since he could never take it for longer than ten seconds, Nessa knew it wouldn't last long.

"You still want this dick?" Chavez enjoyed playing sex games with Nessa and for some strange reason, she was beginning to enjoy their sick sex episodes. Her pussy was throbbing and at that point, she was willing to put anything in her cavern, even his little dick.

With dizzying views outside their window, city after city thousands of feet beneath them, Nessa straddled Chavez and rode him ferociously. As she did, she came hard several times. The orgasms weren't from Chavez's dick though. They were from the realization that she was headed to the next level of the game.

Chapter-16

It had been a month since Nessa had agreed to Chavez's deal. And just like she had expected, she was reaching a new level. With her interests now spread throughout three different cities, she was constantly busy and constantly making money. She couldn't do it on her own though. She had to include Sidra, Trinity and NaNa more closely. She now had the three of them regularly taking trips up and down the highway, back and forth to New York and Baltimore with their crews, each trip worth hundreds of thousands.

Like Nessa had promised Chavez, she paid him back on time for the bricks she'd gotten on consignment. From there, she bought herself a townhouse in the suburb of Gaithersburg, which she spent over a hundred thousand dollars on top notch furnishing. She then bought herself a black Maserati, which she immediately slapped a set of 26 inch chrome Asanti rims on. Shopping sprees were countless for her and Sidra. Her bedroom's walk in closet was now filled with clothes, shoes and bags. She also placed several hundred thousand dollars in a safety deposit box at the bank while also keeping another hundred thousand in a floor safe in her bedroom.

To top it all off, she laced Sidra, NaNa and their individual crews with .45s and Choppers. Knowing the streets were heartless, she'd be damned if she was going to let her people be caught out there without the proper fire power.

Things between Nessa and Chavez were now heating up also. They'd fucked several more times since their business arrangement. And it was obvious that Chavez wanted a whole lot more from Nessa than just her earning power. He wanted her heart. Unfortunately for him, he had no idea Nessa was four months pregnant.

In the beginning, Nessa wasn't quite sure whether she should let her emotions get involved. Emotions and business can complicate shit big time, she knew. But Chavez just wouldn't let her be. He was constantly surprising her with roses on her doorstep, expensive gifts, and dinner dates in the most expensive restaurants. Nessa couldn't help but finally fall for him.

In spite of the success in such a short time, everything wasn't all perfect though. Trinity had informed Nessa that Brandon had been murdered. No one had any idea who did it, which had Nessa paranoid. She asked Chavez about him, wondering if maybe he'd done something to him. Chavez said he hadn't seen or heard from him, nor had he heard about the murder. Nessa didn't quite trust Chavez's response, but had no choice but to keep moving. Hell, it was a blessing, sort of. As long as her previous dealings with him didn't come back to haunt her she was okay with his death. But one thing about his disappearance Nessa couldn't shake...

Piper came up missing at the same time he did.

Nessa hadn't heard anything from Piper in over four weeks. It wasn't as if she hadn't pulled the disappearance act before, but this time her disappearance was more stressful. It worried her. Nessa remembered the coughing fit her mother had the very last time she'd seen her. She wondered about it. She'd begun having fits like that often. And whenever Nessa asked her about it, she shrugged it off or changed subjects. Now Nessa was wondering hard if those fits had something to do with her disappearance. Nessa had called every hospital looking for her mom, filed a missing persons report with the cops, and called every old friend Piper ever had. Nobody had seen her. She even put a twenty thousand dollar reward out on the streets for anyone who could find her, or contribute any information towards her whereabouts. So far, there were no leads.

On top of all that, Nessa was now flip flopping back and forth again about having an abortion, or keeping the baby. She'd already cancelled two appointments at the abortion clinic. She'd made another for the following week and she was dead set on keeping it this time. The counselors at the clinic told her she had now gotten into the dangerous zone for aborting the baby. If she waited much longer it couldn't be done at their facility.

It was a week before Thanksgiving, and Nessa, Trinity and Sidra were now sitting on her townhouse's glassed-in patio, staring through its floor to ceiling windows out at the home's spacious backyard. The branches of the trees were bare, their leaves now golden and strewn about the beautiful green lawn.

"Nothing new from the cops?" Sidra asked, sipping from her glass of Ciroc.

"Nothing," Nessa answered as she sipped Ciroc from her glass. Even though pregnant, she was still drinking and smoking with no worries about how the unhealthy habits could affect the child inside her.

"Well, I've got my people out looking hard for her. NaNa's folks are doing the same."

"I appreciate it."

"Don't worry about it."

"Can't help worrying. The shit is weird. First we find out somebody blew Brandon's brains out, someone whom I couldn't give three fucks about. Two of our spots got robbed recently, and of course money has mysteriously gone missing that only you, NaNa and Trinity touched. Then my mom goes missing! That's a hell of a coincidence. Something's not right about all of this shit."

Although the money situation had Nessa fired up, she was worried sick about Piper.

Seeing how worried her friend was, Sidra squeezed her

leg and said, "She's going to turn up."

"I'm hoping that's true, Sidra, but something's telling me differently."

"You got any suspicions?"

"Chavez."

"Why?"

Nessa thought back to that day when she'd taken Piper with her to Chavez's. She could still remember the looks he was giving Piper. Something about those looks didn't sit well with Nessa *then*. And they still weren't sitting well with her *now*.

"I don't know," Nessa answered her friend. "It's just something about the way he was looking at her when they met. It was weird, real strange." Shaking her head, she said, "Maybe I'm reading more into it than what it was."

"I think you are. I don't know Chavez like you, of course. But if he's fucking with you as hard as he is now, I couldn't see him murdering your mom. I mean, shit, that's bad for business, don't you think?"

"Yeah, but if he did do something to my mom, I'm going to have to deal with him, business or no business. That's something I can't let ride." She was dreading it.

"Well, before we jump to conclusions, let's give it time and find out exactly where she is first. The last thing you want to do is go accusing a man like Chavez of something that serious."

"Of course."

There was a moment of silence when a knock came from the door. Sidra hopped up to answer then immediately developed a frown when Trinity waltzed in like she owned the place. Sidra always dreaded when Trinity was around. She felt she was mentally unstable and interfered with all the plans she had for Nessa's empire.

"So, everything good with your workers?" Nessa asked Trinity, watching her take a seat, and fire up a cigarette.

"Of course. What about yours?" she snapped.

"My what?" Nessa shot her the evil eye.

"How your workers doing?" she asked sarcastically.

Nessa took offense. "This my shit, Trinity...remember that. You've been acting a little crazy lately. Pump your breaks. I brought you in to help you out, so we could step to your mother, together. But you don't run nothing, okay?"

Trinity just stared at her. Then changed her glare to focus on Sidra who was staring her down.

"Take a picture Sidra, it'll last longer, bitch."

"Fuck you, Trinity. You need fuckin' therapy. Some days you happy, partying, and spending money...then some days you hate the world.

Trinity puffed real hard then blew circles of smoke into the air.

"Look, I run my own shit," she said, referring to Nessa's original comment. "I agreed to link up with you so we could get back at Chetti, but since that doesn't seem to be happening, I may need to rethink things. Besides, I don't get paid enough for this shit."

"Oh boy, here we go," Sidra interrupted.

"Sidra, of course your pay is good in all, since you seem to be stealing right up under our nose."

The room went silent.

Nessa looked at Sidra shadily.

Sidra didn't have a response. She just prayed Nessa didn't believe Trinity.

Then, something unsuspecting happened. Nessa received a phone call she least expected.

"Nessa, I need to meet with you? Cedrick's deep voice radiated through the speaker phone."

Nessa's eyes darted throughout the room, looking at Sidra then back to Trinity. She tried to play it cool but she was in complete shock upon hearing his voice. She wondered if she should tell Trinity he was on the other end but thought against it as Trinity had gone through enough with her family. Telling her Cedrick was on the phone could open another can of worms.

"I'm glad to hear from you but where are you and why

do you want to meet with me?" She asked in a whisper. Trinity looked at her as if she knew who was on the phone which made Nessa anxious.

She would have to deal with him later.

For what seemed like forever, Cedrick just stood in the center of the great room in silence. It had been so long since he'd seen it let alone the rest of the mansion. It looked the same as the many years before, minus the cobwebs and dust. The home held so many memories. In his ears he could still hear the laughter of him, Darien, Luke and Trinity echoing throughout the halls when they were children. He could still remember the games of Hide and Go Seek. He could still remember sitting beside his father at such a young age and being explained the rules of business, the rules of stocks and bonds, the rules of owning property. God, how he missed those days.

"You okay?" Mr. Falou asked him.

He nodded.

Amelia squeezed his hand as she stood behind him. She had definitely been holding him down. She cooked for him, shopped for him, and had become his personal assistant. She made sure he had whatever he needed; and was always there when he needed someone to talk to. And although she was a big girl, far from the type of woman he'd always attracted, she had a heart that had him falling for her. He was definitely learning that when it comes to love, it's what's on the *inside* that counts.

Cedrick began to make his way throughout the mansion with Amelia and his attorney. Through a deal worked out between Mr. Falou and the Feds, he was able to get ownership of the mansion along with one of the family's accounts. Without hesitating, Cedrick then got with a broker and began investing money in numerous stocks. Even after all these years, he hadn't forgotten how to make his money work for him.

As he walked through the mansion, it didn't take long before he reached the room he'd been held captive in. Walking inside it, he stood in the center of it just like he'd done downstairs. And just like his mind had been bombarded by happy memories downstairs, it was now bombarded with horrible nightmarish memories, memories that made him cringe.

"This is the room," he said.

No one could speak. Standing beside Cedrick, both Amelia and Mr. Falou cringed themselves at the thoughts of everything Cedrick had been subjected to in that room.

Unable to take it anymore, Cedrick left the room and headed back downstairs. Reaching the bottom of the staircase, a face greeted him at the foyer, a face he thought for sure was a mirage...

Chetti's.

Cedrick, in disbelief that she had the audacity to show up, stood there frozen. He didn't know what to say. He didn't know how to react. All he did know was that he hated her with everything inside him.

Chetti was standing at the foyer with Mac beside her. Little did Cedrick know, Mac had his hand on the trigger inside his jacket pocket.

For a moment no one spoke.

"What the fuck are you doing here?" Cedrick finally asked.

Giving a smile, Chetti finally asked, "You're not going to give your mother a hug, darling?"

Cedrick didn't answer. He just glared at her.

Chetti attempted to hug her son as if there was no bad blood between them.

"Bitch, if you touch me, I'll stomp your head into the floor," he said.

Mac took a step forward.

Amelia squeezed Cedrick's hand once again.

Mr. Falou watched from the top of the staircase.

Everyone was uncomfortable.

Halting, Chetti smirked. She then shook her head and said, "Just like your brothers and sister; fucking ungrateful."

"Ungrateful?"

"Yes, ungrateful."

"You really are sick in the damn head."

"Where's Trinity?"

"Don't worry about it. After what you did to her, you're lucky I'm not bashing your damn head in right now."

She chuckled. "Darling, I have no worries about you or Trinity doing anything to me."

Mac unbuttoned his suit coat to reveal a gun in a shoulder holster. Luckily, Mr. Falou had already managed to dial 911 while still at the top of the stairs.

"No worries at all," she said.

Cedrick wanted to kill her but he knew there would be consequences. Mac would definitely kill Amelia.

Chetti smiled. Then looking at Amelia and sizing her up, she said to Cedrick while still looking at Amelia, "I see you're scraping the bottom of the fruit cup these days."

"Chetti, watch your mouth."

"Yeah, bitch," Amelia co-signed. "Watch your mouth before you get punched in it."

"Get some fashion sense about yourself, hoe. That shower curtain you're wearing and those damn run over shoes aren't working for you."

Seething, Amelia said, "Bitch, don't push it. I'm about a half a second off your ass."

"Fuck you. Isn't there a bucket of KFC somewhere you should be inhaling?"

Amelia charged Chetti.

Mac stepped in between both ladies just in time, giving Cedrick a chance to pull the gun from his holster, concealed under his pant leg. He held it closely to his side.

"You child molesting bitch!" Amelia screamed as she tried to get hold of Chetti.

Luckily, Mac was able to keep them separated.

"The police are on the way!" Mr. Falou yelled from above.

"Eat a dick!" Chetti yelled from behind Mac. "And Cedrick, put a leash on that big bitch before someone mistakes her for a wild grizzly bear and shoots her!"

"Get out of my house, Chetti!" Cedrick demanded.

Stepping from behind Mac and standing at his side, she asked, "*Your* house?"

"Yes, my fucking house. You're trespassing."

Chetti pulled a gun from her purse causing everyone to stand still. "Who the fuck do you think you're talking to?"

Cedrick didn't answer. His eyes were on the gun. Everyone's eyes were on it.

Aiming the gun at Cedrick's face, Chetti said, "Boy, it was I and your father who purchased this house. It was I and him who grinded in these streets for it, not you. Fuck what you think. And don't think that I give two fucks about you having a gun! I've never been afraid to die!"

Nervous but refusing to show it, Cedrick told her, "No, bitch. Fuck what *you* think."

She cocked the gun.

"Mrs. Bishop, this isn't in your best interest," Mr. Falou said, scared of dying.

"Shut the fuck up!" she ordered. "This is family business!"

He quieted.

She focused her attention back on Cedrick.

"So, am I supposed to beg you for my life or something?" he asked, looking her directly in the eyes. "Am I supposed to be scared now?"

Chetti's eyes narrowed. She stepped closer to him and placed the gun to his forehead. Cedrick allowed it without aiming back at her. After all she'd done, he still didn't want to become a murderer.

"Muthafucka, I could murder you right here and right now."

"Then what are you waiting for?"

Sirens sounded from afar. Chetti knew the police were approaching.

"Don't you hear that?" Mr. Falou shouted!

Chetti knew now wasn't the right place and right time to kill Cedrick. She knew the heat was too heavy…too many witnesses. The Feds would come directly for her. She had no choice but to stand down.

"I didn't think so," he told her. "Mother," he added putting stress on their relationship to one another.

"Don't get it twisted, Cedrick. This isn't over."

"The house is now mine. And in a matter of time, all the family's accounts will be mine also. Everything will belong to me."

"And what the fuck do you think I'm going to be doing? Do you think I'm going to stand by and let you take everything I've ever worked for?"

"I don't give a fuck what you do."

"I *will* have my damn house back, Cedrick, even if I have to kill you to do it. You can mark my words."

"Get out now."

Chetti turned and headed for the door. Reaching it, she turned and said, "Cedrick, this is a very dangerous world. If I were you, I'd watch my back." Glancing at Amelia she added, "You and the people you love could easily get hurt."

Cedrick knew what she meant.

"You step foot in this house again or near anything I love, I'll kill your ass," he promised.

Smiling, she said, "I like promises like that. I'll be sure to take you up on it."

With that said, she and Mac were jetted as the police sirens zoned in closer.

Chapter-17

Lying on his back in the trailer's bed, Luke stared up at the ceiling breathing heavily as he recuperated from the latest session of love making with Pamela. She was now lying on his chest. Both were naked.

Luke had honestly thought he'd lost Pamela after her last visit. He'd honestly thought she would never come back. Before their spat, he had never seen her react to a disagreement the way she did. It honestly scared him. It honestly made him wonder about being alone. It made him fear the possibility. But if he only knew...

Pamela, the Federal Agent, never had his back.

He *was* alone.

"I apologize for how things went during our last visit," he said genuinely, "obviously I'm going through a lot."

"It's cool," she said, kissing his chest and cuddling tightly with him. "I understand."

"No, it's not cool. You've been riding with me ever since this situation jumped off. I'm thankful for that."

"I know you are. You've just got to learn to open up to me. I'm not going anywhere. I'm not planning on leaving you to handle any of this alone. I'm not cut that way."

"Thanks."

Those words, although lies, meant the world to Luke. Pamela was all he had. He'd lost Darien. He'd lost Trinity and Nessa, too. Cedrick never wanted any dealings with him again. And Chetti was possibly the one who had tried to have him killed. Other than Pamela, he was truly by himself in this thing.

Looking at her watch, Pamela asked, "Your deposition is in thirty minutes. Are you nervous?"

"No. I've been trained for times like this."

Luke would be sitting down with Federal Agents to give, in recorded detail, intimate and intricate information on the Bishop family operations, specifically Chetti and Darien's part.

"Have to do what I have to do," he said. "Just don't plan on giving them too much on myself, despite the fact they're basically giving me partial immunity."

Silence.

Luke was in thought.

"Immunity?" Pamela asked, surprised that he thought he would actually walk out a free man. "You walking free once you snitch?"

"No…not at all, but my time will be lessened." Luke lowered his head.

"What are you thinking about, baby?" Pamela asked.

"Nothing," he lied.

"Baby, don't do that. Don't shut down on me. What are you thinking about?"

He sighed stressfully. "Just got a lot of regrets, that's all. Wish I could go back and do some things different."

"Like what?"

Luke thought about Cedrick. It hurt him to know that he could've set him free a long time ago. It hurt him to know that he had played a big part in Cedrick's misery just as much as Chetti and Darien, a misery that Cedrick didn't deserve. He didn't speak on it to Pamela though.

"Luke?"

"Yeah?"

"Talk to me, sweetheart. What's on your mind?"

162

Trinity and Gavin filled his mind. Their faces brought regret and pain.

"You have any regrets about your life?"

"Yeah, I think we all do. Anyone who doesn't is lying. I think we've all done something in our life we wish we hadn't."

He nodded and continued to go in deep thought.

"What are your regrets, Luke?"

"I had a son," he admitted to Pamela.

"What?" she asked in surprise. He'd never told her.

Nodding, he said, "Yeah, I did."

"You said *had*. What does that mean?"

He paused for a moment. Swallowing hard, he answered, "He's dead."

"Oh, God, Luke. How did he die?"

Swallowing a lump in his throat, he said, "I killed him."

Pamela looked at him speechless.

Luke sat up, turned his back to Pamela, and placed his feet on the floor unable to face her. "I killed him," he admitted again while staring into the distance.

Seeing his regret, Pamela sat up and rubbed his back.

"Darien brought him in this life. He brought him in our world, a world I never wanted him to experience because I knew it would be heartless towards him. Being my son wouldn't give him privilege. If anything, it would make him a target. Eventually, that's exactly what it did."

Pamela listened intently.

"Family enemies did something cruel to him, something real bad." As he spoke, he could see Gavin's face. He could hear him begging to be put out of his misery.

Pamela continued to rub his back.

"He laid there crying and begging me to shoot him." Pain filled his voice. "I had to shoot him. I had no other choice. I had to kill him to save him."

Cringing at the thought of a father killing his own son, she squeezed his shoulders and kissed his back.

"Damn." He dropped his head. "Damn, I regret that."

163

"The men who did what they did to your son, did you kill them?"

Luke thought about Pamela's question. Under normal circumstances he would never tell a woman his business. He wasn't built like that; but he was vulnerable, and felt like he had no one but Pamela. Darien was dead. Cedrick and Trinity hated him. Chetti and Nessa had both betrayed him, and all of his workers had pretty much acted as if he no longer existed once he got locked up.

There was no one left but Pamela. "I should've," Luke finally answered. "Darien beat me to it. I've killed my share of men though. Too many to count."

"Did you actually pull the trigger?" She gasped, rubbing his back again.

"Just gave the order," he stated, knowing he'd personally pulled the trigger on tons.

"Dear, God, Luke."

"You said that you wanted me to open up and be honest, right? You said you wanted me to trust you. Well, here it is. I'm not an angel, Pamela. Yes, my mother and brother did a lot. But, in all honesty, I'm just as guilty. I touched just as much cocaine, bribed just as many law officials, killed just as many men. That's the man I really am. But I hope you'll love me for me."

His previous concerns with Pam's loyalty went out of the window. It just felt good to get it all off of his chest, hoping she'd ride out his prison time with him.

Pamela said nothing.

Turning around, he said, "Pamela, I love you. And I don't want to hurt you. But I also want you to know I don't want to be that man anymore."

Placing a hand to his face, she said softly, "I still love you, Luke. Nothing you've said will change that. I'm riding with you through this right or wrong."

Luke allowed a slight smile to slip through the side of his lips. Then the two kissed.

"Got a surprise for you," she told him. She then grabbed

her purse and pulled out a cell phone.

"How'd you get that in here?"

Smiling, she answered, "Finesse."

He chuckled.

"After what happened to you, I figured you needed someone to talk to so I took the time to find someone special to you."

"Who?"

She dialed a number. Seconds later, she handed him the phone.

"Hello?" he asked.

"Luke?" Trinity's voice said.

Happy to hear her voice, he stood from the bed with the phone to his ear. "Trinity, I thought you were dead."

Sounding stressed, she told him, "Been going through a lot since the house was hit. Things have been crazy in my life. Luke, I know I said some terrible things to you but I do love you. I would've never truly wished you in that place."

"Trinity, it's okay. I'm not worried about that."

"I know now you never wanted anything but the best for me. Without you out here, I realize that now."

Luke closed his eyes. A tear fell.

"Despite our differences, Luke, you were the only one I could count on."

"I love you, Trinity."

"I love you, too."

Brother and sister spoke a little while longer and ended their call.

Luke stood there in silence for a moment. He kept playing Trinity's voice over and over and over again inside his head. He'd needed to hear that voice. He needed to know she was alive.

Placing the phone back into her purse and getting dressed, Pamela smiled.

Hugging her, he said, "Thank you, Pamela. You're priceless for that. And I thank you for paying off these officers for all these special privileges. I realize none of this comes cheap."

"I told you I'm not going anywhere. Whatever it takes to get you through this, I'm with you."

The two kissed again.

Luke then got dressed and prepared for the deposition. Several minutes later, a knock came at the door. Opening it and seeing a CO standing at the doorstep, he turned to Pamela. The two hugged and parted ways, she on her way out of the facility and Luke headed to his deposition.

The room was small. Its walls and floors were bleach white. One of the walls held a mirror, a two sided one no doubt. In the center of the room was a square table with two chairs across from each other. Sitting in the center of the table was a tape recorder. Sitting on one side of the table and leaning against a nearby wall were two Federal Agents, one very familiar with Luke's case named Agent Logan. Sitting opposite them was Luke. He sat upright and confident while his wrist were in cuffs, never flinching or shying from any questions.

"And who exactly did the Bishops purchase their cocaine from?" Agent Freeman, a solidly built bald black man asked from across the table.

"Fernando Chavez," Luke answered, glancing at the mirror. He knew someone was standing on the other side observing. He was sure it was more agents.

"Was he the family's only plug?"

"For cocaine, yes. Guns came from other sources."

"Names."

Luke named the family's gun connect one by one. He hoped that each name would shave more time off of his sentence.

"How much cocaine at any given time?"

"No less than fifty keys."

"Who set up the deals?"

"My mother."

"Who purchased them? Who made the exchange?"

"Darien and a few goons."

"What about you? Where were you?"

"Never touched any of it. I stayed corporate."

"The fuck you think?" Agent Logan commented, now standing and leaning against the wall. Aside from his stringy hair, he looked like a military Sargent. "We're stupid? Do you really think that?"

Luke simply looked at him.

Agent Logan began to pace the room. Luke could see him focusing on the two way mirror.

"You expect us to think you never touched a fuckin' thing? You expect us to think you were a damn choir boy, a fuckin' innocent piece of the puzzle?"

"I don't care what you think. I'm telling you what it is," Luke said calmly.

"He's bullshitting with us. I say, fuck a damn deal. Let's send his ass away for the rest of his life along with all the rest of them."

Freeman raised a hand to silence his partner.

Logan silenced but reluctantly. By the expression on his face, he wasn't happy.

"Who else was involved in all of this outside your family?" Freeman asked. "To be moving as much weight as your family was for as long as they were, you had to have had help from cops and possibly city or state government."

"One of the family's primary keys to keeping cops off our ass was one of your own," Luke said. "Brandon Bordain...his mother is a Bishop. He made sure the right people in the DEA and ATF were paid off."

"Give us someone else," Logan fired. "Someone did us a favor and blew his fuckin' head off."

Luke showed no remorse. He just shook his head. He figured Chetti had gotten to Brandon. He knew she wouldn't stop

167

until she got rid of them all.

"The city mayor got a nice healthy check also to keep the police chief occupied," he finally fired back. "And several city councilmen filled their pockets with plenty of our money, also; Blake, Hornet, and Williamston," he rattled off.

Logan shook his head in disgust. "Crooked mutha-fuckas," he mumbled.

"Tell us about Chetti kidnapping your brother Cedrick and holding him against his will?"

Luke didn't hesitate. He told it all, willingly.

"Murders. What about murders?" Freeman asked.

"What about them?" Luke twisted his face into a scowl. He seemed irritated.

"How many did the family commit?"

"Can't count on two hands. Too many."

"Give some names, muthafucka," Logan demanded. "Real situations. Real events."

Luke went into detail about several murders, but of course withholding certain information.

"And you?" Freeman asked.

"What about me?"

"How many times did you pull the trigger?"

"Not what I do. My hands stay clean. All I did was han-dle the legitimate stuff, the corporate side of things."

"You sure about that?" Logan asked.

"Of course."

Freeman leaned back into his chair, and looked over at the mirror. He then sighed and looked at Luke again. "Mr. Bishop, I've got reason to believe you're not being completely honest with us about your involvement in the family business."

"Look, I'm telling you what I know."

"Which is a bunch of bullshit," Logan barked.

"Luke, we're taking everyone down," Freeman told him. "That may even include you if you don't want to be honest with us. We don't deal in bullshit."

"I'm telling you exactly what I know," Luke said.

The agents said nothing. They just looked at Luke. He returned their looks. Then while still looking at Luke, Freeman raised a hand and signaled towards the mirror. Seconds later, the room's door opened. When it did, Luke paused. He refused to turn around for fear of what his nose caught.

The smell.

That smell he knew so well.

When he turned to see who was entering. His mouth nearly dropped to the floor when he saw who it was.

Pamela.

Luke was bewildered for a moment. He looked from Pamela to the agents as she closed the door. He then watched as she tossed her FBI badge on the table in front of him and then leaned against a wall folding her arms across her chest. "Surprise, baby," she said. "Shit happens!"

Luke stood up and lunged for her, falling to the floor. "You bitch!" he shouted, wiggling, attempting to stand. His handcuffs prohibited him from moving without difficulty. Luke couldn't believe he'd been played by Pamela; a chick.

This was the woman he cared for and trusted, although he knew better than to trust anyone. This was the woman he'd chosen over Nessa. This was the woman he'd given large sums of money to.

"So, why you? This is how you pigs do things, huh?" He looked at them all as he spoke from his heart about Pamela. "Auction off the pussy for an indictment?"

"It worked, didn't it?" Pamela retorted.

"So, what the fuck does this mean from here?" Luke asked, as the two agents stood him up.

"Well, in the trailer you confessed to crimes that can get you a lot of time for, especially the murder of Gavin Bishop," she told him.

Logan smiled.

"And all those people you just named that were on the Bishop's payroll...we have men headed to round them up now. They'll be snitching on you before the sun goes down; especially after we play the recording of you ratting them out just now."

Luke sighed in regret. He kicked at the two men beside him in anger. "You fuckin' lied!!!!" Veins popped from his forehead. "You told me nothing I said would be used against me?"

"Do you have that in writing?" Logan asked with laughter.

"Jokes on you, Luke," Pamela announced. "In other words, we've got everything and everyone we need. So with all that said, Luke, why exactly shouldn't we lock your ass up for the rest of your natural life?"

"Fuck you, whore!"

"Oh yeah, you'd like to do that one more time, wouldn't you?" She laughed again, before continuing. "Oh, and the money from the 5 Points Deal that you invested is now in the hands of the Federal Government, baby," she grinned wickedly. That was never a real deal. You were investing into a bogus drug company." She laughed hysterically.

Luke just shook his head. If they gave him the opportunity at any point, he vowed to have Pamela killed. It didn't matter that she was a Fed. Her betrayal was so hurtful he was willing to fry if necessary behind her murder.

"Oh and your bitch, Nessa," Pamela continued, "We have strong reason to believe Nessa murdered Brandon. We also have Nessa on video connected to two murders, one of which is the murder of Charles Bishop, your father."

Pamela's voice had someone become muffled. Luke didn't know how to feel. With all of the unsuspecting news he'd become lightheaded. There was too much treachery. And all from women.

He'd allowed pussy to cloud his judgment.

"My father? What the hell are you talking about, bitch?" he asked, both surprised and furious at the same time. He was surprised to hear Nessa's involvement in his father's murder because obviously he had no idea his father and Nessa even knew each other. And he was furious because Pamela had deceived him. He wanted to jump up and break her damn face.

Nodding and smiling, she said, "Yes, your father."

Luke listened, seething. He was seeing red as he stared evilly at Pamela.

Pamela took that as a cue and hurried out to console Cedrick, who was waiting patiently in the lounge area. After viewing his ruthless brother's admission through the viewing window, he had seen and heard enough.

Pam knelt down before his solid, muscular frame, "Cedrick, I know this is a lot to take in but you being here helps us speed up the process and insures we put your brother away for a long time." He held his face in his hands. Even sitting there with an unshaven face and unkempt clothing, he was still fine.

"I think I can help make this situation better," Pam said as she caressed his warm, caramel colored hands. Cedrick could see through her advances but in some way wanted to see where it would take him if he took her up on her offer. Plus, he'd never been with a white woman before.

They locked eyes and Cedrick flirted back, "I will certainly be in touch Agent Pam."

Meanwhile, in the interrogation room, Luke was speechless. He had nothing left to offer. He had no more cards left to play...

Or did he?

Filthy Rich-2 BY: KENDALL BANKS

Chapter-18

The Escalade made its way throughout Washington's rough Belleview neighborhood. Snow fell from the sky and was being brushed away briskly from its windshield wipers. Outside its windows, the temperature was in the low teens.

Although the Thanksgiving holiday had just ended, colorful lights and decorations were sprawled about trees, bushes, lawns and porches. But despite what the cheer and happiness they were supposed to signify, the neighborhood was still what it was. Young drug dealers in bubble coats and Timberlands still stood outside liquor stores serving poison. Prostitutes still sold pussy and sucked dick in piss filled hallways. Every other house was still abandoned. And gunshots still rang out at all times of the day and night.

Sitting in the passenger seat of the Escalade, Nessa stared out at the eyesores with a smirk while NaNa whizzed up and down street after street. Although the people of the neighborhood were going through their struggles and would probably have a miserable Christmas, things were good for her. Business was doing beyond well. Now, on top of having interests in Washington, Baltimore and New York, she and Chavez had now expanded into Detroit and Cleveland. Business and money were growing.

All of a sudden, Sidra broke the monotony of silence that had filled the car for the last ten minutes. "You think Chavez will one day ask you to marry him?"

Nessa turned toward the back of the car to answer but was interrupted by Trinity, "Why would you ask something so stupid like that?"

The two enemies glared at each other for seconds while they both rode in the back seat of the Escalade as if they hated one another.

"I doubt it," Nessa blurted.

"Why's that?" Sidra questioned.

"Because he has plenty of women," Nessa stated firmly. "I'm not stupid. With the type of money he has, I know he has plenty of pop offs all stashed all over the country."

"Maybe," NaNa finally decided to join in. "But evidently he sees something more in *you* than them. I mean, shit, he's putting you in charge of his expansion into new cities, and hired your ass a personal bodyguard. I mean a nigga don't give that type of power to just *any* bitch."

Trinity rolled her eyes and simply got real quiet.

"Right," Sidra co-signed. "And what about the trips and gifts?"

Chavez had taken Nessa to Paris and Jamaica over the last month. He'd bought her furs and jewelry, and had been showing her more attention than what most men show women they like or even love.

"A nigga don't do that type of shit unless there's serious feelings involved," Sidra said, leaning forward, to hit her girl on the shoulder.

Nessa had to smile. "Of course. I know that but..."

"But what?"NaNa asked.

"Shit, after being betrayed by Luke, I'm not sure about marriage. I'm good with the relationship thing but marriage…hell naw!"

"Girl, obviously, Chavez is on a higher level than Luke," Sidra said. "You can't tell me you don't want a piece of that.

Marriage would make it official, and make you the richest bitch on the East Coast."

"Hell fuckin' yeah," NaNa agreed, "Filthy Rich."

Trinity made an annoying sound while blowing her breath, just as the truck began slowing down.

"Look, we're jumping the gun," Nessa told them. "No one's mentioned anything about marriage. Right now, we're just fuckin'. There's a few feelings involved but nothing major. Feelings tend to get bitches nowhere."

Nessa liked her independence. She liked coming and going as she pleased. She liked how things were going right now. Deep down, though, she still didn't trust Chavez. She truly believed he had something to do with Piper's disappearance.

When the Escalade stopped outside a rundown brownstone Nessa perked up. After stopping at the curb, the four of them climbed out of the warmth of the truck and were immediately bombarded by bitter cold. Pulling their coats tighter to their bodies and pulling up their hoods, they headed up the brownstone's walkway. Before making it to the top landing, Nessa noticed what none else had.

A man had quickly crept behind them causing Nessa to react quicker than anyone else. She inhaled, never blinked, and sprang into action. Strapped, she reached for her Chanel which she held underneath her arm, ready to unleash the fire power inside. With her hand on the butt of the .45 she gripped forcefully then released her hold. Thankfully, it was only Joe, the six foot three, solidly built linebacker-looking dude that now protected Nessa daily. With slanted eyes and his naturally long silky black hair pulled into a long ponytail that hung down his back, he was half black, half Asian, and mean as hell. One of Chavez's most trusted goons, he was trained in Martial Arts, and would kill on sight.

"Damn, you gon' get killed running up on me like that!" Nessa fired! "And why the fuck didn't none of ya'll peep him coming! He's fuckin' three hundred pounds! Damn!"

She shook her head pissed the fuck off. She got even angrier when neither Trinity, NaNa, or Sidra responded.

"Wack-ass team," she said conceitedly, before ordering Big Joe to stay out front, watching the spot while they went inside.

Reaching for the knob, NaNa knocked on the door of an apartment with a coded knock. Seconds later, the door opened. A goon with a Chopper in his hand appeared.

"Yo, what up, NaNa?" he asked. "Wasn't expecting you."

"I know," NaNa told him. "Surprise visits is how you keep a muthafucka on their toes."

Nessa, Trinity and Sidra followed NaNa inside, all remaining silent.

The apartment held no comfortable furniture. It only held a few foldable chairs and a television. In the living room, and dining room were numerous tables. Each were surrounded by women who were naked; they weren't even wearing socks. On each table were countless baggies, scales, capsules and piles of cocaine. The women were chopping and bagging everything up.

The walls of both the living and dining room separated the apartment from the one across the hall, and had been purposely knocked down. Because of that, the living rooms and dining rooms of both were now connected to create one huge room. Making their way through the huge room of workers, all of the ladies headed towards the kitchen, following NaNa. As they did, none of the workers looked at them. They stayed focused on bagging the work. Reaching the kitchen, they saw two women dressed in only bra and panties, and like the others standing at two stoves with masks over their mouths. On the eyes of each stove were tall pots of boiling water and cocaine. Behind them, standing at the apartment's back door was a gunman with a Chopper in his hand watching over every movement. On a table and the counters were bowls of baking soda and other ingredients to cook crack.

NaNa and the gunman nodded to each other.

"Everything good?" NaNa asked him.

"No problems," he answered from behind his mask.

"Cool."

"Cool?" Nessa barked. "Why the fuck is it all of a sudden cool for these bitches to defy the rules?" she asked, referring to the only two ladies wearing bras and panties. "When I say stay completely naked that's what the fuck I mean!"

Within seconds, Nessa whipped out her gun and began pistol whipping the young, toothless chick who'd disobeyed the rules of the house. It was crazy for everyone to see how cocky and violent Nessa had become. As blood spilled from the woman's face, Nessa seemed to have no remorse. "Don't fuckin' play with me or my money!" she spat loudly, kicking the woman in the ass with her boot. As the woman stumbled, and attempted to run, NaNa sealed the deal by hitting her with a serious upper-cut that landed the woman flat on her back.

"Worthless ass hoe," Nessa shouted, turning her back.

She wanted to ask Trinity what the fuck she was looking at. But just like the time that had passed earlier, Trinity still said little to nothing. Nessa left the room like a real boss, and ended up back out amongst the rest of the workers. Nessa stood with her comrades in crime and surveyed it all, with her gun still in her hand, down by her side. It seemed surreal for a moment. She had several houses like this one spread throughout the Washington D.C area. There were several more in New York and Baltimore. Now she and her crew were in the process of putting more in Detroit and Cleveland. Nessa had come a long way, she knew.

"Told you shit's all good," NaNa said, hoping Nessa had calmed down. "Paying off the right muthufuckas always pays off."

Nodding approvingly, Nessa told him, "So why does money keep going missing?" She peered into NaNa's face suspiciously with her hands on her hips. "Is it you?" she asked bluntly.

"Me?" In shock, NaNa pointed to himself. "You fuckin' joking, right?"

Nessa's hardened expression said it all. He then looked around only to see Sidra and Trinity gawking at him suspiciously.

"Oh, so this some type of damn set-up? A fuckin trap, huh?" His voice loudened. "After all I did for yo' ass, you now wanna blame me? Bitch, I got money! It's yo' so-called friend!"

"Umph, I've been trying to tell her ass all along!" Trinity finally chimed in.

Nessa's eyes darted back and forth between Sidra and NaNa.

Sidra's hands went up high in the air, and her eyes bulged from her eyes. "Now Nessa this some bullshit. I let it go before when all the accusations started flying, but fuck that! You know I'm down for you! I would never steal from you."

Trinity just crossed her arms glad that the chaos was taking place.

"So, over a hundred thousand dollars has disappeared after we collected from the spots but nobody stole it?"

"I didn't," Sidra blurted.

"If I needed money," I'd take it! I'm fuckin' built like that!" NaNa roared.

Nessa moved her gun in front of her body and smiled. "Nigga, you don't have the heart to take from me openly. Whatever you take, you gotta steal, 'cause you know I'll pop one in that ass."

"Are you threatening me, Nessa?" he asked.

"What it sound like, nigga? Call it what you want!" Nessa gripped her gun, assuring herself that she was ready to go against NaNa if she had to.

"Look, little girl, I don't think you want none of this!"

Nessa thought about the fact that NaNa was notorious for firing down on people, but she knew he had too much to lose. She'd already pressed speed dial on her phone earlier, and had Joe listening on speaker phone. "Joe, we got a disloyal mufucka in here breaking bad. I got this but stay in place just in case he loses his common sense."

"You sure you don't want me to come in, Boss Lady?" Joe's voice echoed loudly.

"Naw," she spoke deafeningly. "It's just a business situation that didn't work out."

"You can't make it without me, Nessa. I helped you build this shit, and I'm the key to makin' it work."

"Nigga, this my shit," she said looking around the house. "Everyone of these mufuckas get paid from my money! And they all getting raises as of today, nigga! You stole from them too, nigga...not just from me!"

Nessa sat her phone down on the nearby table, and grabbed a scale, throwing it against the wall. "Now that I think about it, lots of shit has gone missing...just in smaller amounts; cocaine, money, and even my damn clothes.

"I'm out!" NaNa blurted. With anger in his stride he kicked over several boxes and made his way out of the room and soon out of their house.

"Let him go?" Big Joe soon questioned over the speakerphone.

"Yeah, let that thieving ass nigga go," Nessa sounded.

She looked over at Sidra who had tears streaming down her face. "Ain't no sense in crying now, bitch! We're done. You might as well head on out with NaNa."

"So Nessa, how you gonna do this to me with no proof? she wailed. "I mean damn, don't my word count for something?"

The moment that Sidra heard Nessa cocking her gun, she started backing her way toward the exit door. She had no idea who her friend had become. But she knew that in order to ever have a chance at showing Nessa that she loved her, and that she hadn't stolen from her, it was better if she left. Just before Sidra made it to the door, she turned back around and gritted on Trinity one last time. "Bitch," she muttered as the door closed behind her.

Nessa couldn't believe what had just happened. She had risen to the top of a game where most didn't think she belonged. She'd defied Chetti and Luke, and took over most of their territories, yet she'd just lost her childhood friend. For some reason, she didn't give a fuck about NaNa walking out, but losing Sidra, the only person close to her, other than Piper, hurt like hell. The betrayal had her feeling nauseous.

Minutes later, Trinity and Nessa left the house, and hopped in the car with Big Joe who waited out front as he was told. Nessa thought about the consequences of losing both NaNa and Sidra. They both knew way too much about her personal business.

They knew too much about her drug game.

They knew people she'd paid.

They knew where she kept some of her stash.

More importantly, they both were privy to info that could take her down.

Still in all, "Fuck both of them crooked ass niggas," she shouted to no one in particular. As the car pulled away from the curb, she thought about how much respect she'd gotten from NaNa's recruits over the past few months. She knew with the right amount of money they would surely switch teams. And if they didn't she'd have no problem recruiting some new team players.

Money speaks volumes, she told herself.

She had plenty, and wasn't afraid to handle things alone if she had to.

Nessa's phone rang. With all the chaos going on she didn't pay close attention to the number. "Yeah?" she answered.

Seconds passed.

Nessa said nothing but the expression on her face changed as she listened to the person on the other line.

"What is it?" Trinity asked.

Nessa didn't answer. She didn't even look at her. Shock and worry began to appear on her face.

"What's up?" Trinity asked again.

After several more seconds on the phone, Nessa finally hung up. With glossy eyes that looked like they were about to let loose with tears, she quickly told Big Joe to hop on I-395.

"They found my mother," Nessa said.

"Where is she?" they both asked in unison.

"In the hospital."

Chetti was staring out of the window of her suite at The Four Seasons as she sipped from a glass of Tequila with no chaser. As she sipped, dressed in a satin gown and heels, she heard her phone ring. Seconds later, through a slight reflection in the window, she saw Mac approaching her from behind. "Telephone," he said.

Turning to him and grabbing the phone, Chetti placed it to her ear with downtown D.C under a night sky serving as her backdrop.

"Yeah?" she answered.

"Chetti, I have bad news," Deena said.

"What?"

Sighing, Deena told her, "I'm expecting a new warrant to be issued for your arrest very soon."

"That's preposterous. What the hell are you talking about?"

"Luke has given the Feds everything. He's told them things that weren't included in the original indictments. That means new charges."

Chetti began to nervously pace the floor in front of the window. "That son of a damn bitch!" she screamed.

"I'm sorry, Chetti. I'm expecting the warrant to be issued within the next few days."

"Fuck!"

Mac watched his boss closely.

"What the fuck are you looking at!" she screamed at him. "Can't you see I'm stressed? Refill my fucking drink! Or jerk your fuckin' dick off or something" She took what was left of her drink to the head and shoved the glass towards him.

Taking the glass, Mac headed to the wet bar. He didn't make any expressions at all. In a way he wanted Chetti to get what was coming to her. There were so many things that Chetti had done that he was finally getting wind of.

"Fucking men!" she yelled angrily as she turned back to the window and looked at the golden glow of streaming head-lights and streetlamps. "They're only good for betrayal. I'm sick of their disloyal asses."

"Chetti," Deena said.

"What, Goddamn it?"

"There's something else."

Stressfully running her hand through her hair, Chetti asked, "What is it?"

"Cedrick's working with the Feds also. And from what I hear, they've got something huge planned for both you and Luke."

"What do they have planned?"

"I don't know exactly."

"You don't know?" Chetti screamed furiously. "What the fuck you mean you don't know? Bitch, what the fuck am I pay-ing for? Do more than just prance around looking pretty. You fuckin' incompetent, hoe, find out what the hell they got going on. Find it out now, bitch!" She then hung up the phone.

Mac brought Chetti's drink.

Turning from the window and totally pissed at the cur-rent situation, Chetti saw Mac standing there with her glass in his hand. "What the fuck do you want?"

"Brought you your drink."

Looking at the glass and then looking at him, she swatted the glass from his hand so hard the glass flew across the room. Tequila and ice sprayed everywhere. "I don't want that drink!" she shouted at him. "You made it too quickly. Bring me another one!"

Mac headed back to the wet bar.

"Fuckin', big, stupid muthafucka," she spewed. Begin-ning to pace again she muttered to herself, "A goddamn hundred million dollar per year business gone down the drain. My man-sion is gone, my cars, everything."

Chetti was fuming. Chavez hadn't called her back in weeks, and she was starting to feel like he was holding out. All she had left were the few thousands Mac was hustling up here and there.

"Now, those crooked ass Feds actually think I'm going back to jail? Fuck that. I'll flee the country before I let those muthafuckas send me away. I'll move somewhere where those bastards can't extradite a bitch. I already have a place in mind."

Chetti's mind was running like a machine. As it did, Cedrick's face popped into her head.

Mac once again approached Chetti with a new drink.

"It took you long enough," she spewed, snatching the drink from him. "First, you're too fast. Now, you're too damn slow." She shook her head. "Fucking men!"

Mac didn't speak a word.

With Cedrick on her mind, Chetti told Mac, "Since you can't seem to make a damn drink correctly, get your ass out on the street and do something useful. I want you to put a hit out on Cedrick. Let the streets know I want that muthafucka dead. Offer 300k. But I want to see his dead body, nuts and all. And let me work on getting us the fuck out of the U.S. so you don't fuck it up!"

"Alright," he answered." But how you gon' pay?"

"Don't ask me any fuckin' questions*! I'm not really gon' pay, bitch!* Get the shit done!"

With a doubtful look, Mac grabbed his coat and headed for the door.

Chapter - 19

"How long does she have?" Nessa asked holding her stomach.

"Weeks literally," the doctor told her. "Maybe less."

Nessa was deflated. She felt her heart sink.

"I'm sorry," the doctor told her genuinely as he crossed his arms over his huge belly.

"There's got to be something that can be done. What about Chemo? I have the money. I'll pay for it."

"Chemo treatments won't do any good at this stage. The cancer has spread too far."

Nessa felt destroyed.

"I'm sorry," the doctor told her again. "All that can be done for her now is making her final days as comfortable as possible."

With those words said, he turned and walked away.

Feeling like she was losing her best friend, she signaled for Trinity, and they both headed towards her mother's room. Nessa stepped briskly in a double breasted pea coat, Vera Wang outfit and Jimmy Choo stilettos that clicked loudly against the floor's surface. Her walk, though, was no longer the walk of the old Nessa or an average person. Her walk these days was more of a sashay and glide. Her chin was always raised, chest always out, shoulders always straight, and its speed and rhythm always came off as if she had no time to be held up. She was about business. Power and confidence was more and more becoming a part of her DNA. It was infesting her blood and veins each second so much it now radiated from her.

Beside Nessa was Trinity dressed in Chanel outfit and flats. She walked just as briskly as Nessa. Her eyes were straight ahead as she took each step. She wasn't quite sure about exactly what was going on or why she was there, but never the less, she was going to stick as close to Nessa as possible at all times until her revenge was gotten. Of course, Big Joe wasn't far behind, carrying a Desert Eagle underneath his jacket.

As the three passed room after room, some of the doors were open, others closed. But no matter whether opened or closed, sickness and death was present in each. In a number of the few that were open, family and friends sat near or around their bedridden loved one hoping for the best, pain and even tears in their eyes.

Reaching Piper's room, Nessa told Joe to wait outside. With him doing as he was told and now standing outside the door keeping watch, she and Trinity walked into the room and were greeted by silence. The only sound was the beeping from medical equipment and the front desk nurse's voice occasionally paging someone over the loud speaker.

In bed lay Piper with tubes sticking out of her arms. Approaching her slowly, Nessa couldn't help but be caught off guard by her appearance. It wasn't the fact that Piper had on no make-up that made her look so different. It was the fact that the makeup and certain outfits had been so successful at disguising her mother's disease, she was now unrecognizable. Piper's head was now also completely shaved. Unbeknownst to everyone, the disease had taken her hair a long time ago. She'd been wearing a wig ever since.

As Piper lay in bed with her eyes closed, her frame looked so bony and frail. Her skin looked so dry. Her eyes, although closed, seemed to be sunken into her skull, tiny black mole like spots around their outer edges. She looked nothing like the mother Nessa knew.

Trinity was caught off guard as she herself approached the bed. She'd never seen a person ravaged by cancer. The woman lying in the bed looked to her almost like a skeleton. The cancer had ravaged her body just that badly and just that quickly.

Nessa approached her mother. Standing over her body, her knees almost went weak. Now discovering from the doctor that her mother was near death, Nessa saw the past. She saw memories. She saw the fact that an entire lifetime had passed by so quickly. The realization made her sigh with regret.

Sensing someone near her, Piper opened her eyes. A slight smile appeared on her face when she saw Nessa. Her eyes then looked passed Nessa to see Trinity. The smile immediately dissipated. With almost a sneer, she said in a weak but intense voice, "Get her out of here."

"Mom…

"I said get her out of here. Make her leave."

Nessa turned to Trinity and shrugged her shoulders.

"Now," Piper struggled to shout.

Nessa looked back at Trinity for a few seconds then said, "Wait for me outside."

Trinity frowned but did as she was told.

Now alone with her mother, Nessa turned to her.

"Watch the company you keep," Piper said, with a fearful expression. "Remember, the apple never falls too far from the tree." As she spoke, her body was weak. Just the simple act of saying words drained her of energy. It was a struggle.

"Mom, just because she's Chetti's child doesn't mean she's like her. Trinity is helping me."

Piper gritted her teeth while seething with anger. "I told you hundreds of times, the Bishops are toxic. Everything they touch they destroy. You remember that, Nessa."

"Anyway, why didn't you tell me about the cancer, Mom?" she asked desperately wanting to know about her mother's health.

Piper sighed. Lying on her back, her entire skull nearly swallowed by the bed's pillow, she looked up at the ceiling. Regret, pain and even anger registered on her face.

"Mom, I'm talking to you. Why didn't you tell me?"

"B'cuz, I didn't want a damn pity party."

"But I could've done something."

"There's nothing you could do. This shit is in its final stages. It's been like that for the past year. Nothing can be done for me, baby girl."

Nessa dropped her head. Her heart was hurting. Raising her eyes, now filled with tears, she said in almost a whisper, "You still should've told me."

Both women remained in silence for several moments.

In Piper's head, as she lay there, she saw the day she gave birth to Nessa. She saw the day she'd brought her home. She remembered seeing Nessa take her first step and speak her first words. She saw Nessa's first day of school. Each memory made the current moment more difficult to deal with. Shaking her head, a tear made its way from the outer corner of her eye, rolled down the side of her face and evaporated into the fabric of the pillow case.

Just like her mother, Nessa's mind was in rewind. Saddened, she sat down in a chair beside the bed. As she did, she could remember the lullabies her mother used to sing to her when she was a kid. She could remember playing dress up with her clothes wanting to be just like her. She could remember moments when she, Piper and her father were a happy family. Now, though, all those memories were just that…

Memories.

"Nessa, I've got some things to tell you."

Nessa looked at her mother. She then took her hand. "What is it?"

Sighing, Piper said, "You're going to hate me."

"I can't hate you."

Silence.

The passing of moments.

Mother and daughter looking into each other's eyes.

Nessa took her mother's hand into her own. "It's okay," she assured her, a tear rolling down her cheek to her mouth and leaving a salty taste. "Nothing could make me hate you."

"So many regrets, baby," Piper stated shamefully.

Nessa's knees wanted to buckle. She really wanted to know what her mother was going to say.

"Want to know what my biggest regret is, baby?"

"What is it?" Nessa asked.

"That I won't get a chance to see the happiness *your* secret is going to bring you."

Nessa didn't know what secret she was speaking of. "What secret?"

Piper didn't answer. She simply gave her daughter a smile. It was then that Nessa knew exactly what secret she was speaking of. "How did you know?"

"I know my baby. I know my daughter."

Mother and daughter stared into each other's eyes. Piper then, although extremely weak, removed her hand from Nessa's and placed it softly on Nessa's stomach. Then she went on to spill more beans.

"Nessa, I knew Brandon," she blurted out.

"What do you mean?"

"I mean I knew him."

Nessa didn't quite know what her mother meant.

"I knew him intimately."

Nessa looked at her mother peculiarly.

"Nessa, the two of us had been in a situation for a while now."

"What do you mean *situation*?"

Piper paused. She then finally said, "He and I were sleeping together."

Nessa's bottom jaw dropped.

"You fucked Brandon?" she asked loudly.

"I'm sorry, baby."

Nessa wanted to throw up. The thought of her and her mother fucking the same man nauseated her terribly. Anger built inside her at the news also. Snatching her hand away from Piper, she asked, "What the Hell do you mean?" Nessa's eyes squinted with disbelief.

"Nessa, I'm sorry."

Nessa shook her head and dropped her eyes to her lap.

"That's not all," Piper added. "He and I were working together during the entire time you were setting up the Bishops."

Raising her head, Nessa asked, "Why Mom? Why? And why didn't you tell me?"

Piper paused again.

"Damn it!" Nessa yelled. "Why the Hell didn't you tell me?"

"Because I didn't trust you."

"What?"

"I'm sorry, but I didn't trust you. I had to have Brandon keep an eye on you. I had to be sure you weren't going to betray me. You were too attached to Luke, fuckin' dick whipped, so I had to keep an eye on you."

Nessa couldn't believe what she was hearing. Glaring evilly at her mother, she stood. Shaking her head, she walked across the room to the window and looked outside, her back to Piper. She stared down at the parking lot but blankly.

"Nessa, I'm sorry."

"You didn't trust *me*, huh?" Nessa said with her back still turned. "Ain't that a bitch? You get me involved in this set up, which I myself didn't want any parts of. You lie to me about it. But *I'm* the one who can't be trusted."

Piper felt terrible.

Silence filled the room again.

"If he were alive I would gut his ass," Nessa fired. She was preparing to tell her mother about the news of Brandon being found murdered until Piper spoke.

"I killed Brandon's trick ass, Nessa."

Nessa turned around in shock. Her jaw dropped.

190

"I killed him. I knew I had to," she reiterated. "I knew if I didn't, he was going to mess everything up. I couldn't let that happen. I killed him and the Mexicans. He came clean about killing your dad, too, Nessa. I could not let him live just off that news. I may not have loved your father but he was still your father." Piper had a feeling that Nessa already knew about her father's murder by Brandon but she would never come clean about it.

Nessa placed her hand over her mouth then rushed to the door. She peeked out to make sure no one was listening. Quickly, she rushed over to her mother's bed. "How'd you do it?"

"I fired down on him and that muthafucka, Londo. They was playing you, baby!" She began coughing hysterically and motioning for Nessa to hand her some water.

Nessa handed her the water gently and watched her mother take small sips.

"Brandon had them damn Mexicans rob you. It was all a set-up."

Nessa just shook her head in disbelief. She couldn't believe she'd been so stupid. "I have a question, Ma."

"What is it?"

"If you weren't lying on your deathbed, would you be coming clean about you and Brandon?"

Piper didn't answer.

"Would you now trust me?"

Piper still didn't answer.

Both women just stared at each other across the room.

The answer to Nessa's question was obvious to them both.

A tear rolled down Nessa's face. Her heart was broken. Another tear fell. More fell. Through their veil, she said, "I did this all for you, mama. I did all of this because *you* asked me to. I did it because it was the only thing that seemed to make you proud of me."

"Baby, I was always proud of you."

"Stop fucking lying!" Nessa screamed. "You were never proud of me. The only time you were was when you were getting me involved in your damn bullshit!"

A tear rolled down Piper's face.

"I didn't want to be there when you killed Charles. I didn't want any parts of it. This was all you!"

More tears streamed down Piper's face.

"You selfish bitch!" Nessa yelled.

"Damn it, I made you rich, Nessa!" Piper yelled back. "I made you powerful!"

Piper began to cough. She coughed so hard their force reverberated throughout her entire body shaking the bed. She had no energy left in her, no fight. The cancer was taking it all away.

Looking at her mother and seeing her in such a weak state, Nessa thought about what she'd just told her. She then said, "Yes, mother, you made me rich and powerful." She then headed for the door. Reaching it, she turned to her mother and said, "But look at what it cost us."

With that said, she exited the room leaving Piper alone. Now by herself and with a heart filled with so much regret, Piper cried harder than she'd ever done before in her entire life. Exhausted from the argument, she was able to whisper one thing, one thing she wished she had whispered to Nessa before she left…

"Don't trust Trinity at all. She'll be the death of you."

Nessa stormed out of the room, only to look down at her phone to see an anonymous call coming through. She'd been getting them frequently over the past few days with the caller simply breathing. "What do you want, Luke?" Nessa screamed loudly.

"Pump your brakes, it's me, Cedrick. We still on for the meeting?"

Nessa was silent the entire ride home. She couldn't get her conversation with her mother out of her head and now she had Cedrick to deal with. It just kept playing over and over and over again. It had her stressed and saddened terribly. She was still in a state of disbelief at it all.

In the backseat of the Escalade, Trinity sat silently. As she stared out at the streets from behind the window's dark tent, she herself played back every word of the conversation between Nessa and Piper. Unbeknownst to Nessa, Trinity, while out in the hallway, had been standing by the door listening to every word; especially the news about the pregnancy. She'd surely use it against her soon.

When the truck pulled up in front of Nessa's, Trinity said, "Nessa, I need to talk to you."

"Not now, Trinity. I'm stressed."

"It's important."

Sighing, Nessa asked, "What is it?"

Glancing at Big Joe, Trinity said, "It's private."

Big Joe looked at Nessa.

"Wait in the house," Nessa told him.

Doing as he was told, Joe climbed out of the truck and headed in the house. As he did, Trinity climbed out the backseat of the truck, headed to the driver's door and slid inside.

"So, what is it?" Nessa asked.

"I'm sorry about Piper."

"I don't want to talk about that."

"I understand."

A pause.

Silence.

Then...

"Nessa, this may not be the right time to tell you but there are some things about Chavez you need to know."

"What do you mean?'

"He's not what you think."

Nessa was listening intently.

"He's in bed with Chetti."

193

"What?"

"My mother and he go way back. He was looking at doing a whole lot of prison time years ago. Chetti kept him out though. She could've easily snitched but she didn't. Instead, she gave him money to get himself on his feet. With that money, he built his empire. Basically, without her, he wouldn't be who he is today. Now he's indebted to her for it."

Nessa didn't know what to say or how to react. First, her mother's secrets. Now Chavez and his damn secrets. What the fuck?

"Chavez was the one who stole your money," Trinity continued. "He's been playing you. He even put Big Joe with you to keep an eye on you not just for safety but so he can report back to him everything you say and do. Big Joe is his mole."

Nessa was speechless.

"Chavez even tried to recruit *me*, Nessa. When I was alone with him, he offered me a job."

Nessa was totally shocked.

"He even knows you're pregnant. He's known for a while now."

Hearing enough, Nessa said, "Pull off."

"What?"

"Pull off, Goddamn it!" Nessa yelled angrily.

Trinity put the truck in drive and pulled away from the curb.

"Why didn't you tell me all of this?" Nessa asked, pissed off.

"Because I didn't want you looking at me like you couldn't trust me. I figured you'd probably judge me guilty just by association. I had to prove to you I'm not my mother, I'm not Chetti. I didn't want you looking at me sideways."

"So, you fucking keep all this a damn secret?"

"Nessa, you don't understand. I love you. I love your ass like a fucking sister. From the first time I saw you and we spoke, I saw you like the sister I always wanted but never had."

What appeared to be genuine honesty dripped from Trinity's words. What appeared to be genuine love and compassion dripped from the expression on her face.

"You know I've never quite had a family, Nessa. I just didn't want to take a chance on losing the only thing close to family I have."

Nessa said nothing. She turned her attention to her window. Staring out at the darkness, her mind filled with a million thoughts. What a damn night this turned out to be. She could feel a headache coming on.

"Nessa…"

"Just don't say anything else to me right now, Trinity, okay? Just drive. That's all. Just fucking drive."

Trinity didn't say anything more. She continued driving just like she was ordered.

With the back of her head resting against the headrest, Nessa thought about her father of all people. Killing him had her now in regret. She felt what Trinity had just said about not wanting to lose family. She herself had pretty much lost everyone she considered family. Her father was dead. Her mother was dying. She'd turned on Luke. NaNa was out of the game. And even Chavez wasn't who he had seemed.

Nessa was alone.

The baby in her stomach crossed Nessa's mind. This cycle just couldn't continue. Betrayals, lies, back stabbing, games, murder; these things just couldn't continue. She couldn't take it. It was too much.

As the SUV made its way through the streets, Nessa did a lot of soul searching. Her mind roamed. In the end, she realized she wanted out. She didn't want to stay in this game for too much longer. With that realization, she gave herself a number; 6,000,000. Six million dollars was the amount of money she was going to hustle for from this point forward. Once she reached it, she, her baby, and hopefully her mother if she somehow survived and despite her lies, were going to leave the game and the city. Shit, they would possibly leave the country. Once they did, they were going to start a new life. But first, though…

Revenge.

Chavez couldn't get away with his treachery. He couldn't get away his lies and with stealing Nessa's money. He had to be dealt with.

"We're going to deal with Chavez's ass," Nessa told Trinity. "He's going to pay for crossing me."

Trinity nodded in agreement. "I'm with you." Trinity then called Cedrick to keep him abreast of everything. Although he didn't approve of Trinity's method of revenge, he couldn't stop her.

Chapter- 20

It was nearly 4:30 a.m. The sunrise was still over a couple of hours away. Underneath the darkness and behind an old, abandoned, weather beaten warehouse, dozens of tented out SUVs, and Impalas; each with Government plates, were parked. Among the vehicles were over fifty Federal Agents, each wearing jackets with the words FBI written across the backs. Underneath their jackets were bullet proof vests. All of them also had fully loaded guns in their holsters. With a cold breeze and low temperatures blanketing them, clouds of breath repeatedly appeared in front of each of their faces and slowly evaporated.

The morning's earliness and cloud of darkness was the FBI's favorite time to pull a raid. At this time of morning, most of the world was in a deep sleep, even the criminals. The last thing they would expect at this moment was a group of agents kicking their door in.

In front of the dozens of agents was Pamela. She wore no makeup. Her hair was tied back and tucked underneath a cap. She was dressed in a pair of jeans, Reebok Classics, and FBI issued jacket. Underneath her jacket was a vest and Bureau issued fully loaded .45. In her hands were copies of the arrest warrants for Chetti, Mac, Piper, Nessa, Chavez, and NaNa.

"Now keep in mind that every last one of these individuals is armed and dangerous," Pamela told the agents. "Every last one of them has either killed or been suspected of killing. They're to be taken very seriously. Once you've made entry, never take your eyes off any of these individuals."

The agents nodded to the leaders of each individual unit, holding copies of the arrest warrants in their hands. None of them were intimidated or fearful though. Raids like this one were an everyday thing. Each of them individually had been on no less than a dozen raids. This was just another day at the office for each of them, so just another day that many of them were casually sipping coffee and eating donuts.

Everyone had already been filled in the day before on who exactly they were getting ready to arrest and why: Chetti- Murder, Money Laundering, Racketeering, Drug Distribution, Drug Trafficking, Mac- several counts of Murder, Nessa- The murder of Byron, Accessory to the murder of Charles Bishop and also a host of Drug Charges including Drug Trafficking and Distribution, Piper- The murder of Brandon and Londo, Chavez- Rico Law violations, several murders, Conspiracy, Drug Trafficking, Gun Trafficking, Bribing Law Officials, Running a Criminal Enterprise and a whole lot more.

"When every unit reaches their spot, you don't raid until my say so," she said. "We hit each spot at the same time. I don't want any of these sons of bitches able to call ahead and warn anybody that we're coming. Is that understood?"

Everyone nodded once again.

"Any problems, hit me immediately. Alright, lock and load, ladies and gentlemen."

Everyone checked their weapons one last time and made sure their vests were properly strapped up.

"Alright, folks, let's roll out."

With that said, Pamela headed to a black Tahoe with several other agents and slid into the front passenger seat. The other agents climbed inside with her. As they did, the rest of the agents in her unit climbed into their vehicles also. Altogether, there were five units, each with no less than twenty five agents.

Underneath the morning darkness, the engines of every vehicle came to life, the headlights came on, and their wheels began to roll. With gravel spurting from underneath the tires, each vehicle headed towards the street. Reaching it, each individual unit parted ways and headed for their assigned raid spot.

Pamela, with her radio in hand, looked out her window at the houses passing by. She thought about the investigation. A smirk appeared on her face. It had taken a long time to get all her ducks in a row. Finally, now The Bureaus' patience had paid off.

Everyone was going down.

As the SUV made its way underneath the streetlamps, Pamela thought about the conversation she'd had with Cedrick and Trinity recently. Cedrick, specifically felt Nessa had just simply been caught up. She'd been used by her mother and also Chetti and Luke. And after all she'd done to help him, especially discovering his imprisonment; he felt she should be given some sort of deal, some sort of decreased time. Pamela didn't quite agree. But, because of Cedrick's compassion, she decided to head the unit in charge of raiding Nessa's home so she could be sure nothing bad happened to her.

Reaching Nessa's spot, Pamela's unit approached and parked quietly. Shutting off their engines and killing their headlights, they sat under a cloak of darkness and waited for the other units to check in.

"Unit One in place," the first unit came over the radio.

"Unit Four in place," the next unit finally came over the radio.

Within several more minutes, the other units checked in.

Satisfied, Pamela climbed out the truck and ordered everyone to approach their targeted spot. With her own unit behind her, she approached Nessa's home with her gun drawn. Reaching the door, she silently signaled several of her accompanying Agents to go around back. When they did, she looked at the agent closest to her. Then…

"Go!" she shouted into her radio signaling all units to raid.

The agent standing next to Pamela raised his foot, yelled "FBI", and kicked the front door in. As soon as the door crashed open, Pamela and the other Agents flooded Nessa's home. Greeted with darkness and silence, they quickly made their way through the apartment with their guns out. They made their way from room to room. Pamela herself headed up the steps directly to the bedroom anxious to put the cuffs around Nessa's wrists. Reaching the room and seeing the door closed, she yelled, "FBI, Nessa!"

BOOM!!!!

She kicked the door in. Immediately afterward, she and another agent rushed inside. Heading directly to the bed with their guns aimed, both were disappointed to see Nessa wasn't lying in it. Hopping on the radio, Pamela asked her Unit, "Does anyone have anything?"

"Nothing," someone responded.

"Shit, search every fucking where. Flip the furniture. Check the closets and damn cabinets. Shit!"

Pamela then began hitting the other units. The first to respond was the unit in charge of hitting Chavez's mansion. "You're not going to like this," she was told.

"What do you mean?"

"I think the suspect was tipped off."

"What?"

"Not only is there no one here, but the place is clean from top to bottom. There's no furniture, clothing, nothing. The closets and cabinets are even empty. Looks like he got out of here shortly before we arrived."

"You're fucking kidding me," Pamela said angrily.

"I wish we were."

"Fuck!" she yelled.

Immediately, Pamela hit Chetti's unit.

"Neither of the suspects are here," she was told, speaking of Chetti and Mac.

"What the Hell do you mean they aren't there?"

"They're gone. Looks like they packed up pretty quickly...they knew we were coming," the voice added.

Pamela was now seething with fury. Someone in the Bureau had tipped off everyone. "God damn it!" she screamed.

Without giving Pamela too much time to dwell on her anger, NaNa's unit hit her. "Shots fired. Shots fired," the words came through the radio. "We're taking fire!"

"What the Hell's going on there?" Pamela asked.

"The suspect is shooting at us!"

"We're FBI!" someone shouted in the background. "Stop shooting and lay down your weapon!"

Crack!!!!!

Crack!!!!!

Crack!!!!!

Crack!!!!!

The gunshots were sounding off through the radio like firecrackers.

"Fuck you!" NaNa could be heard yelling.

Crack!!!!!

Crack!!!!!

Crack!!!!!

The gunshots wouldn't stop going off.

"I want that bastard alive!" Pamela yelled into the radio. "Shoot to wound or maim but do *not* shoot to kill. You hear me? Do not shoot to kill. I want that bastard to see his day in court!"

More gunshots.

Pamela listened intently. She didn't even blink.

"Officer hit. Officer hit!" someone screamed.

"Do not fucking kill him!" Pamela yelled into the radio again over the gunfire and pandemonium. "If you hit him, give his ass CPR. Give him the fucking Heimlich Maneuver. I don't give a fuck. And get an ambulance in route immediately. Just don't let that muthafucka die!"

The gunshots continued going off like firecrackers and landmines.

Finally…

"He's down. The suspect is down!"

Anxiously, Pamela asked, "Is he alive?"

No answer.

"God damn it, is the suspect alive?"

Silence.

"Unit Three, come in. Is the suspect alive?"

Seconds later…

"Sorry, sir," a response finally came through. "Suspect's dead. Took a head shot."

Pissed off completely and unable to contain her rage, Pamela threw the radio across the room into a wall so hard it broke into dozens of pieces.

Nothing had gone according to plan.

Chavez was exhausted as he climbed off of Nessa and lay on his back breathing hard and staring up at the ceiling. The two were at a cheap motel outside of Washington.

As soon as Chavez was tipped off about the pending raid, he made arrangements to get out of town. Without telling Nessa about the raid, though, he simply invited her out for one last fuck before he left the country. Afterward, he would head to the next state where he had a private jet waiting. He would hop on that jet and leave America behind.

When Nessa arrived, she made sure to step to Big Joe to ask him one simple favor; leave her and Chavez alone and uninterrupted for their meeting. She even said she would throw him ten stacks for the gesture. He obliged and waited outside in the car.

When she walked in the room, it was silent, except for the sound of a burning cigar.

Lighting up a Cuban cigar, Chavez heard his phone vibrating on the nightstand. Grabbing it, he saw a text notification.

He opened the notification.

Jet Gassed Up And Ready, the text read.

Pleased, he sat the phone back down on the nightstand and took a hit of the cigar. Exhaling smoke to the ceiling, he thought about his homeland, Columbia, the place he was headed. It wasn't everything that America was but it would do. He'd lay low until the heat blew over. Hopefully, he would be able to come back to America one day.

"Why do you love me?" Nessa asked interrupting Chavez's chain of thought.

"Why do you ask that?"

Curling up closely beside him and resting her head on his chest, she said, "Just going through some things right now. I need to hear your words."

Feeling he had Nessa wrapped around his finger, he rubbed her head and said, "Because you're much more than just beauty. You're much more than just a pretty face. That's difficult to find in my line of work."

Nessa listened while staring at the darkness of the room.

"You have ambition," he continued. "You believe in going out getting what you want with no fear of getting your hands dirty. I like that. But above all, there's one thing that truly made me fall in love with you from the very beginning."

"What's that?"

"Your intelligence. You're definitely the smartest woman I've ever met."

Smiling, Nessa raised her head from Chavez's chest, kissed his lips and slipped out of bed naked. Slowly, she made her way across the room to the window but not before grabbing her purse from the floor and pulling out a small case. Dropping the purse, opening the case, she pulled out a pack of cigarettes and fired one up.

As Nessa walked, Chavez watched in admiration of her curves. He watched the sway of her hips, the swing of her ass. It was a shame this was most likely the very last time he was going to fuck her. It had been fun while it lasted.

Reaching the window, Nessa pulled the curtain open, leaned a shoulder against the wall and took a pull of her cigarette. Staring out the window, she saw Big Joe asleep in the driver's seat of the Jaguar parked outside the room. The side of his head was resting against his window. Sighing, she said without turning around, "My intelligence, huh?"

Smiling and placing a forearm underneath the back of his head, Chavez said, "Yes, I truly love that about you."

Still, without turning around, she said, "Then I'm pretty sure you can understand my dilemma."

"Dilemma?"

"Yes."

"What is it?"

"I hate when people underestimate my intelligence."

Chavez didn't quite know what she meant. "Elaborate," he said.

"Like right now. Moments like this one."

"I don't follow."

She turned, holding her purse. Facing him, she said, "Like when a man that I truly admire brings me to some cheap motel, fucks me and smiles in my face as if he hasn't been trying to steal one of my closest workers from me, or as if he hasn't been stabbing me in my back for all this time while working with one of my enemies."

The smile slowly began to dissipate from Chavez's face. "Excuse me?"

Nessa didn't say another word. She simply watched Chavez's eyes from the window. She had no expression on her face.

Feeling uncomfortable, Chavez asked, "Nessa, what are you speaking of?"

"You tried to recruit Trinity."

"Huh, what are you talking about?" He chuckled. "Why would I do something like that?"

Nessa said nothing. Once again, she eyed him.

"Come to bed, sweetheart. No more talk of nonsense."

"Nonsense, huh?"

"Yes, nonsense."

"Is the fact that you and Chetti have been plotting behind my back nonsense, too?"

Chavez grew nervous. He attempted to play it off though. Chuckling, he said, "Baby, I don't know where you're getting your facts from but…"

"I know you were the one who robbed me!" she screamed.

"Nessa…"

"I know about you being in debt to Chetti. I know about it all!"

Chavez knew the jig was up. "Nessa, now look," he attempted to explain.

Nessa pulled a .25 from her pocketbook equipped with a silencer.

Chavez's eyes widened. Sitting up, he demanded, "Nessa, put that damn gun away."

Nessa aimed.

"I'm not fucking playing with you."

"Does it look like I'm playing?" Although angry, Nessa's demeanor and the tone of her voice were calm as she now aimed the gun.

"Nessa, you're not thinking rationally right now. Think about this. You know who I am. You know how powerful I am. I represent a lot of money for a lot of important people. If you shoot me, cartels and kingpins from all over the country will be hunting you."

Click-Clack!!!!!

Nessa cocked the gun.

"Damn it, Nessa!"

"I don't take betrayal nicely, Chavez."

"Shit, you act like what I did was personal. It was business. I owed a debt so I paid it. That's all."

Chavez caught himself. "Wait a minute. What the fuck? Bitch, I don't owe you an explanation for what the fuck I do.

Bitch, drop the gun or will have Joe come in here and rip your ass apart!" Nessa laughed, knowing Big Joe was not going to move his fat ass from the car.

"You just don't get it, do you?" she asked while shaking her head. "Your arrogance has you so fucking blind right now."

"Nessa, put the damn gun down now!"

"Bye, Chavez."

Nessa squeezed the trigger. A sharp darting sound left the silencer as the bullet whizzed from its tip and entered the center of Chavez's forehead causing him to fall backwards flat on the bed. With his eyes wide open, he lay there staring at the ceiling. A thin stream of blood ran from the hole in his forehead, trickled down the side of his face and stained the pillow.

After staring at the body for a moment, Nessa felt numb. Calmly, she got dressed. Moments later, she opened the door of the room. As she did, a cool breeze rushed inside the room and blasted her face. Pulling the collar of her coat tight around her neck, she headed across the sidewalk to the Jaguar Joe was still asleep in. Reaching the driver's side window, she knocked on it awakening Joe from his sleep. She then signaled for him to roll down the window, waving the ten stacks. Still sleepy, he pressed a button and the window came down. As soon as it did, Nessa brought the .25 in sight and squeezed the trigger twice. Both bullets ripped into Joe's face and knocked him backwards until the back of his head was resting against the headrest. With his eyes staring lifelessly straight ahead, blood ran from the two holes ripped into his forehead.

Nessa stared at Joe for a moment. As she did, she saw the face of the man her father had killed so many years ago. She saw her father's face. She saw Chavez's face. She saw the faces of every dead man and woman she'd ever come across. The memories and scenes broke her heart. This wasn't what she asked for. This wasn't what she wanted.

A white Lexus pulled into the parking lot. Slowly it approached Nessa, its brakes squealing lightly as it slowed. When it reached her, nonchalantly she stuffed the gun into her purse, headed to its passenger side door and climbed in. Awaiting her in the driver's seat was Trinity.

"It's done?" Trinity asked.

Simply staring ahead through the windshield, without looking at Trinity, Nessa said, "Yeah, let's go."

Trinity turned the car around and pulled out of the lot. Seconds later, the Lexus was hopping on the nearest highway's on ramp headed back to Washington.

Filthy Rich-2 BY: KENDALL BANKS

Chapter- 21

The early morning sun was rising. Its rays were beginning to shine down over the streets of Washington. As it did, the Lexus separated from traffic and hit the exit ramp. As it did, Nessa's head was resting against the window as she stared at the outside world with almost a blank stare.

"You alright, Nessa?" Trinity asked. "You sure you're up for this?"

"Yeah," Nessa answered with no emotion. She was just ready to get it all over with. She then leaned forward, opened the glove compartment and pulled out a .380. She'd felt the .25 she had used to kill Chavez and Joe wouldn't pack the type of menacing force she would need to deal with what was coming next. She had to be sure she had something that would ensure her next target would *never* get up again in life.

"While you're asking me if I'm sure *I'm* up to this, the question is are *you* sure *you're* up to this?" Nessa asked, looking at Trinity. "Are you ready?"

"I'm sure," Trinity answered. "I'm definitely ready. I've been ready for as long as could remember. I just didn't know exactly when it would happen."

A bitterness developed inside Trinity. It began to show

on her face. "Luke killed my son."

"What?" Trinity gasped.

"He murdered him in cold blood."

Nessa's mouth dropped.

"My son was castrated. He was tortured. Then he was shot in the head."

"Oh my god."

"I told my family I didn't want my son in that life. I told them I didn't want him involved. Behind my back, though, they brought him in. Then, for whatever reasons, they killed him. Luke pulled the trigger."

Nessa was speechless.

"I hate them. I hate my bloodline. I hate the fact that I'm related to them. So, yes, I'm up to this. Yes, I'm definitely ready."

Nessa looked out at the streets. She felt bad for Trinity. She could relate to what Trinity was going through. Now, she clearly understood why Trinity saw the two of them as sisters.

The car was silent.

Nessa grabbed her phone and called her mother's room at the hospital. After several rings, someone answered. It wasn't her mother though.

"Hello?" Nessa said.

"Yes," the person on the other end said.

"May I speak to Piper?"

"Is this her daughter?"

"Yes."

"Ma'am, you should get here as soon as possible."

Growing worried, Nessa asked, "Why, what's going on?"

"There's been a situation."

"What do you mean? What kind of situation?"

"I can't discuss it over the phone. It's very important you get here as soon as possible."

"Okay, I'll be there soon."

When the call was over, Trinity asked, "What's up?"

"Something's going on with my mom. We've got to

make this quick."

"Alright."

Tears began to well up in Nessa's eyes. As they began to fall, she wiped them away. They wouldn't stop falling though.

Placing a hand on Nessa's shoulder, Trinity assured her, "It's going to be alright."

"I don't want to lose her right now. We've had our problems. She's made her mistakes. But right now, I just want us to make things right between us. I want us to be the mother and daughter we're supposed to be."

"That's going to happen."

"I don't know, Trinity. I don't know."

The Lexus reached the warehouse. As it did, the sun was up fully. Pulling behind the building and parking, Trinity killed the engine. She then reached underneath her seat and pulled out a black .32. Cocking it, she stuffed it underneath her coat and looked over at Nessa who was wiping away her tears. Sighing, she said, "This is it."

Nodding in agreement, Nessa said, "Yeah." She then looked at the door of the warehouse and asked, "You sure she's here?"

"Definitely; my source was able to hook it up. She thinks she's here so me and her can talk. She knows I know a lot about the shit The Feds have on her. As usual, she's going to try and talk me out of saying anything. But fuck that. We're going to murk her ass just like planned."

"Alright."

Both women looked at each other without speaking. Their eyes did all the talking. Their eyes signaled that this this moment would usher in the next level of their friendship, their sisterhood. Like a pinky promise, the two were about to get blood on their hands together. Realizing and accepting that, moments later, they climbed out of the car.

The rusted hinges of the warehouse's door screeched loudly as it opened. Mildew and urine assaulted the nostrils of both women as they entered. As they walked inside, the heels of

Nessa's pumps clicked along the surface of the floor. As she walked, she carried her gun at her side. Trinity did the same. Off in the distance, they saw a person standing off in the distance with their back turned while looking out a window...

Chetti.

Looking around, both women approached her. Yards away and stopping, Trinity said, "I'm here."

"I know," Chetti said. "Even among the piss around this place, I can recognize that cheap perfume of yours."

Trinity rolled her eyes.

Turning around, Chetti said, "You never did have good taste in perfume, fashion or anything else that defines a woman's femininity. Sometimes, I wondered how in the Hell you could be my daughter."

Their voices echoed off the walls of the warehouse.

Eyeing Nessa, Chetti said to Trinity, "This is a family moment. I thought I told you to come alone."

"Surprise, bitch," Nessa said with her gun still at her side.

Smirking, Chetti shook her head.

"Trying to sick Chavez on me was a bad idea, Chetti," Nessa told her.

"Oh, was it?"

"Yeah."

Chuckling, Chetti asked, "And speaking of Chavez, how's my dear friend doing?"

"Dead, the last time I checked."

Chetti shook her head once again. "This business will do that to you, I guess. Well, as long as I got my money's worth out of both him and you, it's not a problem."

"Money's worth out of me? Bitch, please."

"Awwww, sweetie, you didn't know?"

"What the fuck are you rambling about?"

"Nessa, you were grinding for me, baby. You were hustling for me. Shit, you basically worked for me. Every time you paid, Chavez, you were paying me. Shit, even every time you

212

sucked his dick, you were eating my pussy."

Nessa eyed Chetti.

Smiling, Chetti asked, "How does my pussy taste, bitch?" She then laughed.

Nessa angrily cocked the gun.

"Sore loser, I see." Chetti chuckled.

"Oh, I'm not the loser. I'm not the loser at all."

"You're not, huh? Poor thing. Not too bright, neither." Chetti's voice was irking the Hell out of Nessa.

"I guess you thought you were going to fuck your way into my family and take over shit without me checking up on you, huh? I guess you thought I wasn't going to find out who you really were."

Nessa didn't speak.

"Sweetheart, I didn't become the queen of the streets by being slow. You'd better believe I didn't stack my blocks any differently than the rest of the kids in kindergarten when I was a kid. As a matter of fact, I graduated at the top of my class."

"What the fuck does all this mean?"

"It means I'm always ten steps ahead of bitches like you."

Click-Clack!!!!!

The slide of a gun cocked.

Hearing it behind her, Nessa didn't move. She knew she couldn't.

Smiling, Chetti asked, "How's Piper doing? When I saw her in the hospital just recently, she didn't look too good."

Nessa's stomach plunged at now knowing Chetti knew about her mother and where she was.

"Drop the gun," Mac demanded from behind.

Ignoring Mac's voice, Nessa told Chetti, "If you touched my mother…"

"What, bitch?" Chetti asked. "What the fuck are you going to do about it? Is this the moment where you say some dramatic shit like if you touched my mother, I'll kill you? Is that it? Bitch, you ain't Halle Berry and this ain't Hollywood. No matter what I did or do to that tramp ass mammy of yours, ain't a fuckin' thing you can do."

"Drop the gun," Mac ordered again.

Nessa held the gun tighter. She wanted to raise it. She looked over at Trinity to see her standing still also, unable to raise her gun. Both had been stopped in their tracks.

Mac stepped closer. "Drop it or I blow your head the fuck off," he demanded again.

Nessa finally did as she was told.

Trinity didn't.

Mac picked up Nessa's gun. As he did, Nessa was wondering why Trinity hadn't dropped hers and why Mac wasn't demanding that she drop it. Then Trinity looked at her as Mac stepped back with his gun aimed at the back of Nessa's head.

Silence.

Both women just stared at each other.

Then…

Trinity aimed her gun at Nessa.

"Trinity, what the fuck are you doing?" Nessa asked surprised.

"Didn't think I knew, huh?"

"Knew about what?"

"Bitch, don't play fucking stupid!"

"Trinity, I'm not playing. You're like my sister. I'd never hurt you. What are you talking about?"

"You'd never hurt me, huh?"

"No."

"Bitch, you killed my father!"

Nessa couldn't utter another word.

"Yeah, bitch, I know about what you and your mother did. I saw the video. I saw the two of you slice his throat from ear to ear."

Nessa definitely couldn't speak now. Her past had finally caught up to her.

"You sneaky hoe!"

"Trinity, if you saw the video, you know I didn't want

any parts of it. I wasn't the one who killed your father."

"You were there, Nessa. You were there and you did nothing to stop it!" Rage was all over Trinity's face as she screamed.

Chetti was taken aback at the exchange. She was caught off guard. Although she and Trinity had plotted to get Nessa to the warehouse, she had no idea that Nessa had been the person who killed her husband. "Wow, I guess it's true what they say, huh? You really do learn something new every fucking day."

Nessa once again couldn't speak.

Stepping towards Nessa, Chetti said, "Damn shame, huh? You came here expecting to kill me. But what happened? All your own dirty laundry got aired out and the tables got turned." Glancing at Trinity, she then said, "Can't trust anybody nowadays, huh?"

Nessa looked at Chetti with bitterness.

"That's exactly why I killed Darien. Can't trust mutha-fuckas. No matter how good you feed even the most loyal of dogs, they'll pretty much always turn around and bite the *fuck* out of you."

Trinity put away her gun and pulled out a knife. Its polished blade ricocheted in the morning sunlight.

Chetti smiled and took a step back.

"You tortured my father," Trinity told Nessa. "Now you're going to get a chance to see how the shit feels."

Nessa's heart began pumping.

Chetti turned and began to walk away. As she did, she said, "Trinity, I hate to spoil your fun, sweetheart, but I'm going to have to be a real mean bitch right now."

Mac pointed the gun at her.

Not clear about what was going on, Trinity looked at Mac.

"Drop the knife," he demanded.

"What?"

"Drop the damn knife!"

Trinity looked at her mother.

Turning around to face her daughter, Chetti said, "I would advise you to do what he says. Trust me; he can get quite nasty with that gun if you don't."

Trinity dropped the knife.

Mac picked it up.

"We had a fucking deal, Chetti. I brought Nessa here."

"As I said, before, Trinity, you just can't trust people nowadays. I mean this game pays well, *extremely* well. Clearly it made this family rich. But the trust level is just so fucking shitty."

Trinity was pissed.

"Where's Cedrick?" Chetti asked.

"You low down bitch."

"Yeah, yeah, yeah," Chetti said waving those words off. "Miss me with all that. Where's Cedrick?"

"That wasn't our deal."

"I'm putting an end to all this today. You, Nessa, and Cedrick are the only ones left out here who can take me down with the things you know and the things you've seen. All of you have to die."

Trinity was pissed. The tables had been turned on her also. She'd planned to kill Chetti right after she'd murdered Nessa.

"Where's Cedrick?"

"Fuck you!"

Sighing and losing patience, Chetti pulled a gun from underneath her coat, quickly walked over to Trinity and slapped her with the butt of the gun's handle.

Trinity fell to the floor holding her temple. Blood was running from underneath her hand. "You bitch!" she screamed from the floor.

Nessa's body tensed at the sight.

"Trinity, do I look like I have time or that I'm in the mood for your fucking theatrics?" Chetti asked holding the gun.

"Fuck you!" Trinity screamed again.

Shaking her head, Chetti kicked Trinity in the face so

hard her head swung viciously. As it did, blood sprayed from her mouth.

Dazed, Trinity screamed, "I'm going to kill you. I swear to God I'm going to kill you!"

"Where's Cedrick?"

"Go to Hell, bitch!"

Training the gun on Nessa now, Chetti asked, "Where is he?"

"I don't know," Nessa told her.

"Where the fuck is he?"

"I don't know!"

Chetti was losing patience quickly. "Tie them up," she ordered Mac.

Mac roughly tied Trinity up first to a chair. He then grabbed Nessa by the hair and began to force her across the floor to a table. Reaching it, he said, "Lay on the table."

"What?"

SLAP!!!!

The backhand sounded almost like a gunshot.

Nessa dropped to the floor dizzy.

With no patience for Nessa, Mac picked her up, and slammed her down flat on her back on the table so hard the back of her skull thudded causing a massive headache. He then began to tie her up. When he was done, she was tied spread-eagled by her wrists and ankles. He then stuffed a handkerchief in her mouth.

Chetti approached Nessa. Now standing over her, she was holding a broken glass bottle she'd picked up from the floor. "I made a promise to you, remember, Nessa?"

Nessa didn't say anything. She looked into Chetti's eyes. What she saw caused her heart rate to elevate uncontrollably. It caused her to breathe heavily.

"A while ago, I told you that if I ever found out you were pregnant with my son's child, I was going to kill that bastard, remember?"

Nessa began crying. Her eyes raced from the bottle to

Chetti's face.

"Yeah, you do. You remember it clearly. In this family we keep our bloodline in order. No new blood allowed. My next grandchild will be Raquel's baby," she sneered.

Nessa's body began to tremble.

Smiling sickly, Chetti said, "I always keep my promises, thanks to Trinity's info."

Nessa sighed thinking about how Piper had warned her. She was so right.

With that said, she ripped open Nessa's coat, raised her dress and said, "Hold still, baby." The gun that Nessa concealed was now Chetti's for the taking. "Thanks for the gun, too, you dumb whore."

Mac watched while keeping Trinity in his sights.

Chetti, without warning, shoved the bottle inside Nessa's pussy, attempting to perform an on-site abortion.

"Ahhhhhhhhhhhhhhhhhhhhhhh!!!!!" Nessa screamed gut wrenchingly behind the handkerchief in her mouth, its sound muffled. She'd never in life felt pain like this.

"Like that, Chetti?" asked. "Here take some more." She then stuffed the bottle inside Nessa again, this time further than before.

"Ahhhhhhhhhhhhhhhhhhh!!!!!" Nessa screamed again. She writhed wildly in pain.

"Take it, bitch!" Chetti yelled over the muffled screams.

Nessa could feel her insides tearing.

"Take all of it, bitch!"

Chetti began to stuff the bottle in repeatedly and furiously. It, along with her hand, was now covered in blood. The sight of Nessa's blood urged her on. The expression on her face was like that of a rabid dog. "Come on, bitch. Take it!"

Trinity watched silently, her own blood running down the side of her face and from her mouth down her chin. She felt no remorse for Nessa.

Chetti kept ramming the bottle. "Is that bastard child of yours dead yet?" she asked Nessa.

218

Nessa was now crying. She could feel the blood spilling from inside her. She could feel it running underneath her back and staining her thighs.

Chetti finally dropped the bottle. "Told you I was a lethal bitch," she told Nessa.

Nessa wanted to die. So many tears were falling from her eyes she couldn't see Chetti's face clearly. Chetti was almost a blur to her from behind the veil of tears.

Suddenly...

Chetti pulled out the knife Trinity was going to cut Nessa with. "This is for precautions," she said. "I don't like to leave anything to chance." She then brought the knife's blade down into Nessa's stomach.

Nessa screamed once again from behind the handker-chief. Her screams faded as her body slipped into shock.

Satisfied, and leaving the knife in Nessa's stomach, Chetti turned her sights and attention to Trinity. "Your turn now."

"Fuck you!" Trinity yelled defiantly.

Chetti pulled out the gun once again. "Your ass was never fit to carry the Bishop name. Time to dismiss your mutt ass."

Mac stepped in between both ladies.

"Get out of the way!" Chetti demanded. "Can't your dumb ass see I'm in the middle of something?"

"Sorry, can't let you do it," he told her.

Looking at him like he'd lost his mind, she asked, "What the fuck are you talking about?"

"Remember when you said you can't trust anyone nowa-days?"

She didn't answer.

"You were right," he told her. He then aimed his gun at her.

"What the Hell are you doing?" she asked.

"Something someone should've done to your old miser-able ass a long time ago."

With that said, he squeezed the trigger.

Chetti immediately grabbed her stomach as the bullet ripped into her belly. Blood began to leak from underneath her hand. She dropped to one knee. With a surprised look on her face, she looked up at Mac. "You son of a bitch, you shot me," she told him.

Trinity gasped. She was just as caught off guard as Chetti.

"That's a gift from Cedrick," Mac said.

In pain, Chetti said, "What?"

Mac then reached into his pocket, pulled out his cell phone and dialed a number. Seconds later, he pressed the speaker phone button, and sat it near Chetti. With blood all over her hands, she attempted to touch the phone.

"Hello, mother," Cedrick's voice said.

"What the fuck is going on?" Chetti asked him, clearly in excruciating pain. Her voice trembled.

"A little something I like to call retribution. Only took a hundred thousand to make Mac turn on you."

"I should've killed you when I had the chance, Cedrick!"

"Should'ves don't win races, mother."

"You son of a bitch."

"How does it feel to know my voice is the last one you'll hear before you die?"

"Fuck you. I'll see your ass in Hell. I promise you that."

Cedrick laughed.

"You hear me? I'll see you in Hell, Cedrick."

The phone went dead.

Chetti now looked up at Mac. "You ungrateful, mutha-fucka," she sneered.

Ignoring her, he kept the gun aimed.

"Well, what are you waiting for?" she asked. "You think I'm going to beg or something? Fuck you!"

Mac took a step towards Chetti. He then placed the gun to her head.

"Do it," she said. "You spineless, muthafucka. Do it!"

Mac placed his finger on the trigger.

Chetti looked up into his eyes.

Then…

The door to the warehouse flew open abruptly. Federal Agents quickly flooded the building. They'd been positioned outside listening through taps they'd placed throughout the warehouse.

"Drop the gun!" someone shouted.

Caught off guard and not clear about what to do, Mac turned to the agents still holding his gun. As he did, Chetti pulled Nessa's gun out of her pant waist, aimed at the back of his skull and squeezed the trigger. The back of his head cracked open like a watermelon. Immediately, he collapsed to the floor.

"Drop the gun now!" Agents shouted as they quickly approached Chetti.

"Fuck you!" Chetti screamed as she let off a shot.

Gunshots sounded off immediately as the agents opened fire on her. Ducking while still holding her stomach, she dashed up the stairs, moving slower than normal. As she did, she let off several more shots from her gun. A blood trail followed behind her as her blood poured from her stomach. The agents ducked and fired back, one shot successfully entering her leg. However, she kept moving until she reached the top of the stairs and disappeared deeper in to the warehouse. The agents had her now.

Pamela appeared, "Someone get me a damn ambulance here, quick!" Pushing through agents, she rushed to Trinity. "Are you hit?" she asked frantically.

"No," Trinity told her.

She then saw Nessa lying on the table. Immediately, she dashed over to her.

Nessa was now staring up at the ceiling. Blood was running from both sides of her mouth and streaming down both sides of her face while even more blood gushed from her belly.

"Oh my God," Pamela gasped as she immediately placed a hand over Nessa's wound. "Hold on, Nessa. Hold on."

Tears began to fall from Nessa's eyes. She had so many

regrets. So many what if's filled her. Her mother, her dead father, the way she betrayed Luke…and so much more.

Trinity watched with a smirk. She sincerely hoped the bitch bled to death.

"Nessa, hold on. Help is coming." Pamela never wanted deaths on her watch. She wanted convictions.

Nessa couldn't speak. She began to drown in her own blood. Coughing, blood began to spray from her mouth.

"I need a fucking ambulance *now*!" Pamela screamed into her radio.

Nessa's eyes closed.

"Nessa, I need you to open your eyes for me. Help is coming. I need you to open your eyes."

Nessa tried. She attempted to as she thought about the life in her stomach. She tried her hardest, wanting to at least give her child a shot at life if possible. She tried with everything in her will and power to open her eyes.

But…

She couldn't.

"Nessa, open your eyes!"

In darkness, the voices around Nessa seemed to drift farther and farther away.

"Nessa!"

Moments passed.

Then…

Silence.

Nessa's bleeding body lay still as Federal Agents milled about the building, most heading up the stairs to apprehend Chetti and survey her wounds. While they did, Pamela continued to yell at Nessa hoping she could hear her. Her yells and screams, though, were useless…

They were falling on deaf ears.

Then…

"Agents," a voice came over the radio.

"What is it?" Pamela asked.

"We just got word from the prison. You're not going to

believe this"

    "What?"

    "Luke Bishop escaped."

Filthy Rich Part 3 Coming June 2015

CHECK OUT THESE TITLES
BY: Kendall Banks

www.lifechangingbooks.net

In Stores NOW

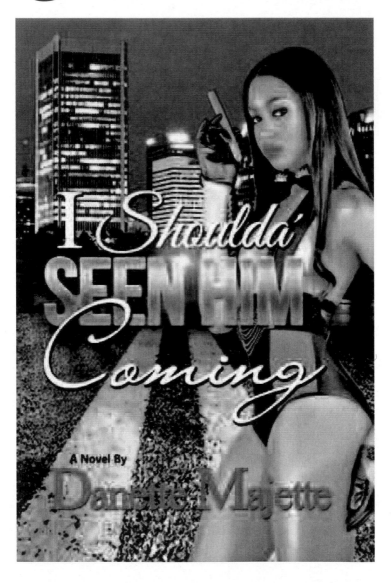

I Shoulda' SEEN HIM Coming

A Novel By
Danette Majette

More Hot Titles

MAIL TO:
PO Box 423
Brandywine, MD 20613
301-362-6508

ORDER FORM

Ship to:		
Address:		

Date:	Phone:

City & State:	Zip:

Email:	

Make all money orders and cashiers checks payable to: **Life Changing Books**

Qty.	ISBN	Title	Release Date	Price
	0-9741394-2-4	Bruised by Azarel	Jul-05	$ 15.00
	0-9741394-7-5	Bruised 2: The Ultimate Revenge by Azarel	Oct-06	$ 15.00
	0-9741394-3-2	Secrets of a Housewife by J. Tremble	Feb-06	$ 15.00
	0-9741394-8-7	The Millionaire Mistress by Tiphani	Nov-06	$ 15.00
	1-934230-99-5	More Secrets More Lies by J. Tremble	Feb-07	$ 15.00
	1-934230-95-2	A Private Affair by Mike Warren	May-07	$ 15.00
	1-934230-96-0	Flexin & Sexin Volume 1	Jun-07	$ 15.00
	1-934230-89-8	Still a Mistress by Tiphani	Nov-07	$ 15.00
	1-934230-91-X	Daddy's House by Azarel	Nov-07	$ 15.00
	1-934230-88-X	Naughty Little Angel by J. Tremble	Feb-08	$ 15.00
	1-934230820	Rich Girls by Kendall Banks	Oct-08	$ 15.00
	1-934230839	Expensive Taste by Tiphani	Nov-08	$ 15.00
	1-934230782	Brooklyn Brothel by C. Stecko	Jan-09	$ 15.00
	1-934230669	Good Girl Gone bad by Danette Majette	Mar-09	$ 15.00
	1-934230707	Sweet Swagger by Mike Warren	Jun-09	$ 15.00
	1-934230677	Carbon Copy by Azarel	Jul-09	$ 15.00
	1-934230723	Millionaire Mistress 3 by Tiphani	Nov-09	$ 15.00
	1-934230715	A Woman Scorned by Ericka Williams	Nov-09	$ 15.00
	1-934230685	My Man Her Son by J. Tremble	Feb-10	$ 15.00
	1-924230731	Love Heist by Jackie D.	Mar-10	$ 15.00
	1-934230812	Flexin & Sexin Volume 2	Apr-10	$ 15.00
	1-934230748	The Dirty Divorce by Miss KP	May-10	$ 15.00
	1-934230758	Chedda Boyz by CJ Hudson	Jul-10	$ 15.00
	1-934230766	Snitch by VegasClarke	Oct-10	$ 15.00
	1-934230693	Money Maker by Tonya Ridley	Oct-10	$ 15.00
	1-934230774	The Dirty Divorce Part 2 by Miss KP	Nov-10	$ 15.00
	1-934230170	The Available Wife by Carla Pennington	Jan-11	$ 15.00
	1-934230774	One Night Stand by Kendall Banks	Feb-11	$ 15.00
	1-934230276	Bitter by Danette Majette	Feb-11	$ 15.00
	1-934230299	Married to a Balla by Jackie D.	May-11	$ 15.00
	1-934230308	The Dirty Divorce Part 3 by Miss KP	Jun-11	$ 15.00
	1-934230316	Next Door Nympho By CJ Hudson	Jun-11	$ 15.00
	1-934230286	Bedroom Gangsta by J. Tremble	Sep-11	$ 15.00
	1-934230340	Another One Night Stand by Kendall Banks	Oct-11	$ 15.00
	1-934230359	The Available Wife Part 2 by Carla Pennington	Nov-11	$ 15.00
	1-934230332	Wealthy & Wicked by Chris Renee	Jan-12	$ 15.00
	1-934230375	Life After a Balla by Jackie D.	Mar-12	$ 15.00
	1-934230251	V.I.P. by Azarel	Apr-12	$ 15.00
	1-934230383	Welfare Grind by Kendall Banks	May-12	$ 15.00
	1-934230413	Still Grindin' by Kendall Banks	Sep-12	$ 15.00
	1-934230391	Paparazzi by Miss KP	Oct-13	$ 15.00
	1-93423043X	Cashin' Out by Jai Nicole	Nov-12	$ 15.00
	1-934230834	Welfare Grind Part 3 by Kendall Banks	Mar-13	$15.00
	1-934230642	Game Over by Winter Ramos	Apr-13	$15.99
	1-934230618	My Counterfeit Husband by Carla Pennington	Aug-14	$ 15.00
	1-93423060X	Mistress Loose by Kendall Banks	Oct-13	$ 15.00
	1-934230626	Dirty Divorce Part 4	Jan-14	$ 15.00
	1-934230596	Left for Dead by Ebony Canion	Feb-14	$ 15.00
	1-934230456	Charm City by C. Flores	Mar-14	$ 15.00
	1-934230499	Pillow Princess by Avery Goode	Aug-14	$ 15.00
			Total for Books	$
		Shipping Charges (add $4.95 for 1-4 books*)		$
		Total Enclosed (add lines)		$

* Prison Orders- Please allow up to three (3) weeks for delivery.

Please Note: We are not held responsible for returned prison orders. Make sure the facility will receive books before ordering.

*Shipping and Handling of 5-10 books is $6.95, please contact us if your order is more than 10 books. (301)362-6508